The

Woman

Who

Walked

on

Water

Lily Tuck

Riverhead Books

NEW YORK

1996

The

Woman

Who

Walked

on

Water

RIVERHEAD BOOKS
a division of G. P. Putnam's Sons
Publishers Since 1838
200 Madison Avenue
New York, NY 10016

Library of Congress Cataloging-in-Publication Data

Tuck, Lily, date
The woman who walked on water / Lily Tuck.
p.   cm.
ISBN 1-57322-021-3
1. Women—Fiction.   I. Title.
PS3570.U236W66   1996
813'.54—dc20   95-808 CIP

Printed in the United States of America
1   3   5   7   9   10   8   6   4   2

This book is printed on acid-free paper. ∞

Book design by Jennifer Ann Daddio

My thanks and *shukr*
go to Amy Hempel,
Alexandra Harding,
Cindy Klein Roche,
and Celina Spiegel.

To my mother
and to Julie:
good friends

I was reading a story of Tolstoy's at the Tolstoy Museum. In this story, a bishop is sailing on a ship. One of his fellow passengers tells the bishop about an island on which three hermits live. The hermits are said to be extremely devout. The bishop is seized with a desire to see and talk with the hermits. He persuades the captain of the ship to anchor near the island. He goes ashore in a small boat. He speaks to the hermits. The hermits tell the bishop how they worship God. They have a prayer that goes: "Three of You, three of us, have mercy on us." The bishop feels that this is a prayer prayed in the wrong way. He undertakes to teach the hermits the Lord's Prayer. The hermits learn the Lord's Prayer but with the greatest difficulty. Night has fallen by the time they have got it correctly.

The bishop returns to his ship, happy that he has been able to assist the hermits in their worship. The ship sails on. The bishop sits alone on deck, thinking about the experiences of the day. He sees a light in the sky, behind the ship. The light is cast by the three hermits floating over the water, hand in hand, without moving their feet. They catch up with the ship, saying: "We have forgotten, servant of God, we have forgotten your teaching!" They ask him to teach them again. The bishop crosses himself. Then he tells the hermits that their prayer, too, reaches God. "It is not for me to teach you. Pray for us sinners!" The bishop bows to the deck. The hermits fly back over the sea, hand in hand, to their island.

—DONALD BARTHELME

The

Woman

Who

Walked

on

Water

One

*God's grace is the beginning, the middle and the end.
When you pray for God's grace, you are like someone
standing neck-deep in water and yet crying for water.
It is like saying that someone neck-deep in water feels
thirsty, or that a fish in water feels thirsty, or that
water feels thirsty.*

—RAMANA MAHARSHI

The first time I saw Adele, Adele was swimming in
the Caribbean. She was swimming the sidestroke
with three big dogs swimming alongside of her. Irish
setters.

Everyone eating in the expensive restaurant on
top of the cliff—including the waiters—was
watching her.

Adele swam so far out to sea that the water was

no longer a friendly azure but a dark navy blue and so far out that her head and the heads of the three dogs were just little dots on the horizon. And when, for a minute, I stopped looking at Adele, I stopped following her progress to look down and make sure there were no bones left in my fish, it was hard, when I looked back out to sea for her again, to tell which one of the four dots was Adele.

The people in the restaurant with me—between mouthfuls of fresh-caught grilled red snapper—said to each other things like: *That woman must be crazy! That woman must be suicidal! I don't care how strong a swimmer she is! Doesn't that woman know about sharks?* I heard one person say: *Those poor dogs! It's inhumane to treat dogs that way! It's inhumane to make dogs swim out that far! What if one of those poor dogs drowned?*

By the time I was halfway through the passion fruit and mango flavors, my favorites, of the three-flavored-sorbet dessert, Adele had started to swim back to shore. It was easy for me then to distinguish which of the four dots was not a dog's head but Adele's.

The darker dot.

After shaking the water from their long coats, the setters had lain down panting in the sand, while

Adele was already jogging back toward the oleander and palm trees growing at the edge of the beach. I was sipping espresso, and I saw Adele throw something—a stick, maybe—but the dogs only made a halfhearted attempt to retrieve it for her. Afterwards, their tails and belly hair heavy with wet sand, the dogs trotted slowly after Adele, back to her bungalow, and it was clear to me watching from above in the restaurant that Adele was the one who still had plenty of energy left.

Two

I probably should say that I have Lily. Later, after I got to meet Adele, Adele told me the names of her three dogs: Heidi, Suzy, Lily. Three bitches: mother, daughter, sister. Lily is twelve years old now. Her coat is almost as soft and as long and as shiny as it used to be. I make sure her teeth get cleaned, so that she still enjoys her food (unless it is a certain kind of dried food). In the summer in the country, she likes to chase after squirrels. The most noticeable change that has occurred is that Lily has become hard of hearing. She cannot always hear the doorbell ring, or hear me turn the key in the lock when I come home in the evening.

Lily! I have to shout at her if I want her to sit or stay or obey me.

I probably should also say that Lily, the dog's name, was the reason I turned around and spoke to Adele in the first place. Lily sounds so much like my own name that when Adele had called out to her dog, I mistook it—perhaps, too, on account of the noise of the wind blowing and of the waves breaking, I could not hear distinctly—and I thought Adele was calling out my name.

A coincidence, I said to Adele, but Adele right away answered that there were no such things as coincidences. Coincidences, she told me standing there on the beach, were miracles.

Lily, Lily! What in the world happened to Adele? from time to time I still say to Lily in my new loud voice.

Three

I did not mention the bathing suit Adele was wearing. A red two-piece bathing suit. The kind of bright red you can see a mile away, the kind of bright red a matador's cape is made out of so that the bull will charge it, a red like the red and purple and orange of the bougainvillea that was growing alongside the cliff on which the expensive restaurant where I was eating my red snapper was situated, a red Mark Rothko painted before he painted nothing but black. In other words, a red I, personally, would never be caught dead in.

I was wearing my blue one-piece bathing suit; even so, the French boy said he noticed the difference right away. The French boy—he wore nothing but a bikini bathing suit and white sunscreen cream on his nose and he rented out the masks and the flippers and he took care of the boat so that the people staying at the resort could go waterskiing—went on to say that in spite of the way Adele and I were standing together with our hands on what-do-you-call-them-in-English? our *hanches,* and the way we had both pushed up our dark glasses, our *lunettes de soleil,* on top of our heads, Adele's hair was *court* and curly, my hair was longer and lighter, Adele's *visage* was oval-shaped, mine was *plus rond,* and he was also talking about how Adele was at least half an inch taller than I was and how Adele weighed at least *cinq ou six* pounds *moins* than I did (Adele had lost so much weight in India; the food there, she said, the spicy food went right through her).

"Adele, where in the world did you learn to swim like that?" was one of the first things I wanted to know.

7

Adele had shrugged her broad, swimmer's shoulders. Standing next to me on the beach, in the red two-piece bathing suit, she was still dripping wet. The three dogs, Heidi, Suzy, and Lily, were lying panting at her feet.

Adele claimed she learned how to swim before she learned how to walk. Her father had taught her. In the shallow end of a neighbor's pool, her father had walked alongside of Adele, his hand under her stomach supporting her. He was talking to her, and at some point her father had removed his hand, Adele said, but he kept right on walking and talking. Adele never noticed, Adele kept right on floating.

Adele said she was naturally buoyant. Some people were; others sank to the bottom like stones. For instance, Howard, her husband, did. Even in salt water, even in this beautiful blue Caribbean Sea, Howard, Adele told me, always had to tread water.

One time, when she and Howard were first married—how many years ago? how many years had they been coming to this same beach resort?—Howard had tried to keep up with Adele. Half a mile out in the ocean, Howard had had to turn back. He just then remembered, he told Adele, that he had made an appointment to telephone his office. Never again did Howard swim so far out with Adele.

On the other hand, Nina, Adele's daughter, admitted right away that she got frightened. At a certain distance from the shore, Nina told Adele, she would start to feel panicky—she could not help it. Nina said she had a feeling—the opposite of claustrophobia— that the shore was too far way and that she would never reach it. However hard or fast Nina swam toward it, the shore stayed the same distance away, and Nina, by anyone's standards, Adele said, was a strong swimmer.

As for Harry, her son, swimming, Howard was right. Harry was lazy. Harry preferred, Howard said, to lie on the beach and sunbathe.

"I've always been a little afraid of the water, I've always had a healthy respect for the ocean," I said to Adele then. Adele was looking out to sea, I am not sure she was listening to me.

"I used to swim a lot in school, too. In high school," Adele told me. "I went to swimming meets all over the state—my father used to drive me himself. He wouldn't let me go in the bus with the other kids. He said the other kids were not serious. Sometimes, he would drive all night, while I slept in the back seat of the car—a green Studebaker, I'll never forget that old car—and if I won, my father would stop off at a bar to celebrate."

"And if you didn't win? If you lost?" I said.

"C'mon, Suzy! Heidi! Lily! Time to go!" Adele called to the three dogs. Obediently, the three dogs rose from where they were lying in the sand and, close to her heels, trotted after Adele.

Four

When the angel falls in love,
He is the perfect human.

—FARIDUDDIN ATTAR

"According to the book I am reading, there are ninety-nine attributes," was one of the first things Adele said to me. In the same two-piece red bathing suit, she was sunbathing on the beach, and the way she lay on her back her hipbones jutted out like two sharp sticks. As I pulled up a chair, I noticed a book, its pages covered with sand, lying next to her.

"You mean attributes like honesty? Like charity?

Is that what you mean, Adele?'' I was not sure how to answer her. Looking away, I watched the steady progress of a small sailboat on the horizon.

"The hundredth attribute is a secret,'' Adele continued, crossing her long legs the other way. "Only after an individual has acquired the ninety-nine attributes can he or she learn the hundredth attribute. The secret attribute.''

"Let me see, I said honesty, I said charity, which makes two already. What about a sense of humor—that's an attribute, isn't it? That makes three. What else? Bravery makes four, patience makes five, independence is six, cleanliness is seven, generosity is another attribute, which makes eight. Any positive quality, I guess, is an attribute. I could go on and on.''

I watched as the small boat's sails flapped in the wind, then as the boat tacked and changed direction.

"Yes. Imagination, sensitivity, courage—''

"Courage is like bravery, and I said bravery already, but imagination and sensitivity are different, which makes ten. God, it's hot here. Aren't you hot, Adele?''

"Intelligence makes eleven. Probity makes twelve—no, you said honesty, didn't you? Charity? Have you said charity? Charity makes thirteen.''

"Adele, you are not listening, charity was the second attribute I mentioned. At this rate we will never get to ninety-nine. What about sexuality? Do you suppose sexuality is considered an attribute? Maybe, just a little bit of healthy sexuality, which would make it what? Thirteen? Fourteen?"

The sailboat had rounded the end of the peninsula, I could no longer see it.

"I've lost track," Adele answered. "For some reason, I can only think of their opposites—greed, avarice, vanity, gluttony, lechery, treachery, and of course, adultery—oh, God, don't remind me." Smiling, Adele shook her head.

"You mean like synonyms—fidelity, loyalty, devotion. Do they count as three or as one?"

"Verdad, veracidad, honradez, probidad, integridad," Adele said.

"Oh, you speak Spanish!"

"I'm going in. I'm going for a swim."

Adele, I soon learned, had a habit of not answering. When I looked over at her again, Adele was already walking down to the sea.

"Swimming!" I called out after her. "That's it, isn't it! The hundredth attribute! The secret attribute!"

"Here, Heidi! Here, Suzy! Lily!"

The three dogs, who had been lying on their sides in the shade of the oleander bushes, got up and trotted over to Adele. Adele, her back to me, her hands on her sharp hips, was standing waist-deep in the water waiting for them.

Shading my eyes with one hand so I could see her better, I watched Adele swim. Occasionally, her feet splashed a bit of spray up in the air. The ocean was a dark blue that afternoon and full of slapping little waves. Some of the waves had whitecaps, which made it harder for me to follow Adele's progress.

I looked and I looked and kept looking until I could no longer see Adele and the three dogs; then I went over and looked at her book.

Five

I don't remember whether it was Nina or Harry who persuaded me. But it must have been Nina. (Before Lily, I had never owned a dog. I once owned a cat, a beautiful chocolate-colored Burmese cat with unblinking gold eyes that I named Belle Star, and after Belle Star died, I vowed that I would never again own another animal.) It certainly was not Howard. Howard said he did not give a damn by then, and Howard was already living with someone else. And this was after Heidi got run over by the UPS truck and after Suzy either ran away or was kidnapped. I remember that Nina said how both she and Harry had put advertisements in the local newspapers, how they put up reward signs on the telephone poles in the neighborhood, all to no avail. Nina said that now Lily would surely die of a broken heart if I did not take her (Nina would have gladly, only her landlord did not allow dogs in the building) and how, after all, I had been Adele's friend, hadn't I?

Six

According to another book that I have been reading recently, there are two opposing theories concerning ''only'' children. The first maintains that the only child is more motivated because he or she gets more of the parents' love and attention and has a better chance at a college education; the second theory says that an only child tends to be introverted, introspective, and less motivated because he or she does not benefit from sibling rivalry to develop a healthy competitive spirit.

Adele's personal theory on the subject of only children was that neither of these two theories applied to her. Her case was different, she said.

Early on, Adele developed a solipsistic theory that only she existed. Everyone else—absolutely everyone—Adele said, existed only for her benefit. Adele's parents, Adele's friends, Adele's *aya* (the reason she learned Spanish), Adele's big brown poodle, Hasan (Adele's theory included animal, vegetable, mineral), were present only if Adele was there; otherwise they vanished, they disappeared into thin air. Plane crashes, coups d'état, earthquakes, the self-immolation of priests, the birth of quintuplets—the more sensational the news item, the better—took place only to fill Adele's head with information.

If she was clever, if she was always attentive, Adele was convinced that she could catch this "emptiness." For a brief half second, perhaps, she could get a glimpse of this nothing, this *nada,* of the way the world was—the way the world *really* was—without her. In the street, Adele would deliberately turn a corner too fast or on a crowded sidewalk, she would stop dead in her tracks and quickly look back. She would do the opposite of what she had set out to do, of what was expected of her: front was back, left was right, walk was run.

She wanted to fool, to surprise, to outsmart.

At home, her parents, she said, either indulged or ignored her. They believed what Adele told them. Her father believed Adele when she said she had not laid eyes on his bottle of imported gin. Her mother believed Adele when she answered: *Only the radio!* the time she heard a male voice inside Adele's bedroom and through the shut door called out: *Adele! Are you in there?*

Adele left college after one year. She wanted to travel, she said. Already, she argued, she spoke Spanish. Now, she would learn French. Her parents tried to dissuade her; Adele, in an effort at compromise, said she would take courses at the Louvre Museum. But the whole time Adele was living in the Quartier Latin, she only once crossed the Seine (Adele had to go to the American Embassy on the Avenue Gabriel to fill out the form for a new passport—she claimed she had lost hers, when in fact, she had sold it).

Adele was lucky.

Adele did not get caught the time she stole a baguette, Adele did not get caught the times in Paris she rode the bus without paying the fare, Adele did not get caught the time she was hitchhiking alone in France and trespassed by camping out overnight in a farmer's field, and in the morning, when she woke up, she found the farmer's German shepherd guard dog lying on top of her sleeping bag eating the salami, bread, and cheese that Adele kept in her knapsack. The canvas knapsack was ruined, the German shepherd had chewed through it. The farmer, when he discovered Adele, invited her over to his house where his wife gave Adele coffee with hot milk in it and grilled bread with homemade honey that tasted of clover. Adele said how, for as long as she lived, she would never forget the taste of that honey. As for the German shepherd, the farmer and his wife told Adele, he was young, not trained properly, harmless. In the future, they would keep the German shepherd chained at night. They hoped that Adele had not been frightened by him.

Everywhere Adele went that year—Zurich, Florence, Rome, Taormina, Athens, Marrakesh, Tangiers, Barcelona, Lisbon, London, Land's End—her address was always the same: care of general delivery, American Express. Adele, however, rarely went to pick up her mail.

Instead, she would send a postcard of Capri from some place in Greece, the name of which was obliterated by the illegible postmark, or else she would phone from a remote post office where she would either be disconnected or be unintelligible.

For a whole year: *Où est Adele? Dov'è Adele?*

When Adele came back, she had lost fifteen pounds, bought a new set of clothes, cut off her long hair, and still spoke no French.

Seven

Miracles are the menstruation of men.

—KWAJA MIR DARD

But speaking of French, Adele said, France was where she met Him. Adele met Him inside Chartres Cathedral.

"Who? Who did you meet?"

Adele and I had walked from the beach—Adele walked faster than I did, I had to half run to keep up—past rows of small wooden houses painted pink, blue, green. The narrow streets of the Caribbean village were crowded with tourists shopping for straw hats, baskets, rum, duty-free items. Adele had an errand to do—first thing, she said, she wanted to buy decent shampoo (in India, her hair had gotten dried out, had gone almost white).

And on the day that she met Him, Adele said, she started to hiccup. She could not stop, she said.

"Met who?" I tried asking her again.

For three days and three nights, Adele hiccuped. She could not sleep and her chest hurt so much it was painful for her to breathe. Also, she got frightened. Her father had started to hiccup—a sign, sometimes —the day before he killed himself drinking gin.

In front of a shoe store, Adele suddenly stopped. She pointed in the window to a pair of sandals with thick wedge cork soles. (Back home in Connecticut, Adele had a closet full of shoes, and she had bought, she said, a pair of those mesh see-through shoes long before they became fashionable.)

I said, "When would you wear those shoes, Adele?" (I had pictured Adele walking along the banks of the Ganges River. In those sandals, precariously balanced on those impractical wedge cork soles, Adele, I imagined, would have to step over excrement, over the bodies of the dead.)

Adele said, "Shall we go in? Shall we take a look for just a minute?"

In the end, after trying on several different pairs of shoes, we each bought espadrilles—not the sandals with the thick cork soles on display in the window but canvas slippers with rope soles to wear on the beach. The espadrilles were so cheap—they cost four dollars each—that Adele bought two pairs. Size $8^1/_2$. We had, it turned out, the same size feet.

When we were outside in the street again, Adele told me how she had to hold her breath, how she had to drink upside down from a glass of water, a glass of Coca-Cola, of white wine, of Armagnac, how she had to eat a teaspoon of sugar, eat a teaspoon of salt, of crushed garlic, of anise seeds, of spices she could not identify and that tasted bad; how everywhere she went, someone had a remedy that had always worked for them and did not work for her. Adele did everything she was told to do and everything she could think of, including—she got so desperate—nearly scaring herself to death by walking on the narrow parapet on the roof of their hotel.

It got crazy, Adele said. Three whole days in the Loire Valley and she could not stop hiccuping. Adele hiccuped her way through Chenonceau, Blois, Amboise, and the prettiest château of all—Azay-le-Rideau. Everyone—the other tourists, the guides—must have thought she was drunk.

And during this time, all she could think about was death, about dying. Strange deaths. Violent deaths. Dying too young. In retrospect, Adele said, this was natural because a seeker believes that he is born again when he meets his teacher.

One last thing, Adele said she nearly forgot to mention. On account of the hiccups, she and Howard could never make love. The one time they tried—the day they visited Amboise and Blois—Adele had spoiled it by starting to laugh.

"Adele!" This time I shouted. "Who are you talking about?"

In the busy Caribbean village street, holding the package with the two pairs of espadrilles in it and turning toward me to speak, Adele went, *Hic.*

Eight

Adele said she liked swimming on her side best. She liked the feeling of her arms stretched in opposite directions, her face half in, half out of the water, her legs extended, toes pointed, coming quickly together. She especially liked the feeling that she was displacing a mass of water, moving it, rearranging a bit of the ocean. Each time she stroked, she pressed an armful of water away from her chest; each time she kicked, she squeezed more water from in between her legs.

When Adele was so far out to sea that no one on the beach could see her, sometimes she would take off her two-piece bathing suit. She would continue swimming the sidestroke—often, she would change sides then—holding the two pieces of red nylon and Lycra in one hand.

The three dogs, Heidi, Suzy, and Lily, always swam alongside of Adele in the ocean. One dog would swim on either side of Adele—Heidi and Lily, say, while Suzy swam slightly behind them, or the formation might change, and Suzy and Lily would swim beside Adele while Heidi would be the one swimming a few feet ahead of them. No matter what their grouping, the three dogs always stayed fairly close together in the water; one dog never lagged behind the two others, one dog never swam further out or faster than the two others, one dog never turned around to swim alone back to the shore.

Nine

This Self is the honey of all beings
and all beings the honey of this Self.

— THE UPANISHADS

In a quiet—relatively speaking, since in India no place is truly quiet—residential section of a medium-sized city (smaller than Bombay or Madras), a city the size of, say, Bangalore or Benares, in a neat white house with closed wooden shutters and dried-out looking palm trees growing outside, was where Adele said He lived.

Except during the rainy season (the season when

Harry came out to visit her), it was always hot there. On a typical morning, the rusty thermometer nailed to the house registered 112 degrees Fahrenheit. It was so hot that two mongrel dogs stuck together in the street were lying down. It was so hot that Adele no longer heard the sound of a car horn blowing at syncopated intervals: *Nah nah, nah nah nah, nah nah, nah nah nah.* It was so hot that in the kitchen the ice cube was melting on its way from the refrigerator to Adele's glass.

His house was always filled with people: His family, His relatives, His friends—and with seekers like Adele. His house was always filled with the noise of people talking, men arguing, babies crying, women running water, washing, and filled with the smells of curry, garlic, jasmine, incense, sweat.

In the living room the whirring of the ceiling fan barely displaced the warm air where, every afternoon, about a dozen people—mostly men—would already be sitting cross-legged on the wooden floor waiting for Him. They were meditating, they were *remembering* God, a few of them were in deep *dyana,* in a trance.

When finally He would enter the room, it was, Adele said, as if an unseen wind had suddenly banged open a shutter, knocked from its stand a vase with a flower. He would move rapidly across the room to His chair. He was wearing a long white *kurta,* a *dhoti.* Like everyone else in the room, He was barefoot. His feet were strong, the nails were cut short and square. Without looking right or left or at anyone, He sat down.

The room was hotter still. The air was like thick hot steam. It was hard to breathe. The slightest movement—a shifting of weight, a straightening out of a shoulder blade, a slight clenching or unclenching of the jaw—made the heart race, beat louder, beat irregularly. On His left, the young man dressed in jeans had a sudden headache, a pain like a jab of a knife behind his eyes. To His right, seated almost hidden from view in the back of the room, the bearded old man could hear the buzzing of a thousand bees in both his ears. Sitting directly in front of Him, Adele both shivered and felt feverish.

After a few moments of silence, He began to chant softly from the *Ramayana.* Even in the gathering dusk, His face shone and was suffused with so much light that no one dared to look directly at Him. His eyes sparkled more brightly than precious stones, more brightly than any stained glass.

Then all of a sudden, through an open window, a

cat jumped into the room—an ugly, black and yellow alley cat. Without pausing or breaking its stride, the cat jumped directly into His lap.

The cat had made Him laugh. A hearty belly laugh. A loud merry laugh. The kind of laugh that Adele said she had not heard in a long time. The kind of laugh her father used to laugh when she won.

Ten

Adele—Howard was the first to say so—was spoiled. It had cost Howard a small fortune: the plane tickets for the three dogs (the price is calculated according to the weight, and my guess is that each dog weighed at least fifty pounds), which did not include the cost of the three large kennels, and Howard had not even mentioned the trips he made to the veterinarian to get the three dogs their shots and their health certificates.

But what else was Howard to do? He had promised Adele, he said.

And Adele always got what she wanted. From the very beginning, hadn't Adele told Howard how she wanted one boy, one girl, two dogs (only she ended up with three—who could resist Suzy?), and one horse? Adele was the one who wanted to live in the country (Howard disliked the commute every morning, he would have preferred to live in the city). For their vacations, Howard said, Adele always insisted on going to the same beach resort in the Caribbean where she could swim.

Not only was she spoiled, Howard was to tell me on the day I went to his office, the same day I saw the framed photograph Howard still kept on his desk of Adele—Adele in her running shorts with the number 1855 pinned to her T-shirt and one of her arms raised up in the air with her fingers spread out in a V—Adele was lucky.

Howard was not talking here about anything special ("No, no," he said, "Adele did not win the lottery!"), but Howard was talking, for instance, about how when Adele drove into the city, no matter how crowded or busy the streets, right away she managed to find a parking place. Or if Adele was caught speeding—Adele, Howard said, was always in a hurry, Adele always drove at eighty miles an hour—how she would manage to talk the policeman out of giving her a ticket. Or—and this had happened just a few years ago—when Adele had left her engagement ring, a valuable pear-shaped diamond that had belonged to Howard's mother, on top of the sink in the ladies' room of a restaurant, someone had found it, turned it in to the manager, so that when Adele had gone back to the restaurant (Howard who had been with her had said: "Forget it, Adele. That ring is history!") to look for the diamond ring, the manager of the restaurant, to celebrate—as if finding the ring was not good fortune enough—had offered Adele a free glass of Dom Perignon champagne.

In addition, Adele had a knack of making things work out in her favor—being late resulted in a serendipitous meeting, the same was equally true if she arrived early. If Adele happened to take a wrong turn, the road was sure to lead her somewhere, like the much-talked-about time she took the second instead of the third left after the light and found herself driving past a big horse barn. Of course, Adele could not resist; she had gone straight in. And what else but a sign was the beautiful gray mare with the long swishing tail that happened to be there for sale? Right away, Adele had made friends with the trainer.

But there was no use reminiscing or complaining about it, Howard had given her his word: Adele could spend a week swimming in the Caribbean with only Heidi, Suzy, and Lily for company. In return, Adele had promised to come back to Connecticut.

Actually, as Howard had told Nina, his daughter, at the time, in a way he should have considered himself lucky. He had gotten off lightly. Adele might have asked him to send down her gray mare, Sylvia Plath, as well.

"A goddamned horse. Can you imagine?" was what Howard had said to me then.

Eleven

Besides the sea and the sandy beach, the hotel itself attracted people to the resort. Each whitewashed stucco bungalow—part Moroccan, part adobe-style architecture which blended in with the natural decor —was concealed from the other bungalows by the artful planting of hibiscus, oleander bushes, and other fast-growing tropical trees. The privacy and the simple comfort were what Adele told me she liked best.

Why, she could spend a week there, she said, and never once run into her neighbors.

The bedrooms were airy and kept still cooler by large ceiling fans; the bathrooms were decorated with Italian tiles and amply supplied with clean towels, soap, creams, and bath oils; in the living room, the cushions on the rattan sofas and chairs were covered with crisp patterns of matching blue and green cottons; every day, the flowers were changed in the vases in each room. In addition, as a practical matter, there was a small but serviceable kitchenette. Lastly, each bungalow was built slightly differently. Some bungalows had patios that gave directly onto the beach, others had shady thatched-roofed balconies, still others had walled-in rooftop terraces with a splendid view of the sea—Adele said how she and Howard always requested the bungalow with the walled-in rooftop terrace, where, high above everyone and completely hidden from view, Adele could sunbathe nude.

The food in the restaurant was prepared by a French chef. People came from all over the small island to eat the grilled fish, the native lobster tails, the curried prawns and shrimp dishes, the homemade duck liver pâté, the island-grown salads with the special house dressing—what was the secret ingredient? a dab of ginger? soy sauce in the vinaigrette?—to say nothing of the delicious desserts: tirami su, the mango and passion-fruit sorbets, the special crème caramel.

The service, if not impeccable, was friendly. The waiters liked to stand around with starched white napkins draped over their arms and chat. They could not be rushed. The women who made up the beds and cleaned out the rooms wore wide skirts and petticoats, old-fashioned blouses with bodices. On their heads they tied colorful kerchiefs. They spoke the local patois in singsong voices and laughed when they had to answer too many questions. Each morning, one of the women would arrive with a laden breakfast tray balanced on her head and open the bedroom door without knocking (Adele described one time when she and Howard were still in bed making love—Howard, she said, was much more attentive to her in the Caribbean and she did not need to lie to him, a few times she had actually climaxed!), and the woman would invariably ask them: "So, how are you two folks doing this morning on this beautiful day?"

Twelve

Another thing I remember was how Adele's short hair
—so short, to me it looked shorn—was curly and
dark (except for a few streaks of white in it), and how
it was important for her, she said, to get her hair cut
right. While Adele was living in Connecticut, she had
a standing appointment, once a month, at a beauty
salon in the city. But later, the best haircut Adele was
to get in her whole life, she swore to Howard, was in

Bangkok. In Bangkok, Adele found someone who knew exactly how to cut it. It was luck, it was *karma* —there she was, Adele told Howard, all alone for ten days in Bangkok with the airport closed, the airlines on strike, and nothing to do during the Thai New Year, a holiday, and all the shops were shut except for this one hairdresser shop.

But what did you really do in Bangkok, I mean besides getting your hair cut? Adele's husband, Howard, had wanted to know.

Thirteen

A man swims the Tigris River every night to be with his beloved. One night, for the first time, he notices a mole on the beloved's face. That night, the beloved warns him not to cross the river for he will drown.

— A SUFI STORY

"But what does He look like?" I asked Adele. I tried not to sound skeptical. I tried to sound casual and as if the answer did not matter. "I mean is He tall? Is He handsome? Is He clean-shaven or does He have one of those beards that He wears tucked up under His chin?"

The sky that day was the same cloudless blue, the ocean a lighter, greener aquamarine-blue. Sitting next to Adele on the beach, I was patting one of the three Irish setters. (I have to admit that at the beginning Adele's three dogs, Heidi, Suzy, and Lily, looked exactly alike to me.)

"Oh, God, I don't know," was how Adele had answered me. "He keeps changing, and He has shaved off His beard. Sometimes, He looks very young, very handsome. At other times, He looks a hundred years old, two hundred years old, a thousand years old—and not just His age, His height, too, varies." Adele's voice sounded oddly young, high-pitched. "There are times, you should see Him, when He is so tall that I can pick Him out anywhere. At the airport in Bombay, for instance—the airport in Bombay is so crowded, so chaotic, people yelling, people shouting and begging for money, people trying to carry your luggage, and I only have the one small duffel bag"— here Adele gave a little laugh, the way she would sometimes, "He stands out head and shoulders above the porters, the conductors, the other passengers, above everyone. Yet at other times," Adele's voice sounded lower, more impassioned, "like in a crowded taxi, He can make Himself so small, so tiny, that He takes up less room than His little grandson. One time, in Madras, I swear this is true," Adele paused a moment, then she resumed speaking a little louder than before, as if she were making a particular effort to enunciate or as if she were translating the words from another language, "I nearly did not recognize Him. He looked exactly like a girl. Yes, I swear. A beautiful girl with breasts."

Fourteen

I asked a child walking with a candle,
"From where comes the light?"
Instantly he blew it out.
"Tell me where it is gone—
then I will tell you where it came from."

— HASAN OF BASRA

At the beginning, in India, it was especially difficult for Adele to concentrate. The house was noisy, she said. She never had enough privacy—not even in the bathroom, least of all in the bathroom. Worse still, she never had Him to herself without someone interrupting them—His wife was always coming in the room to ask Him for something, His daughters were forever quarreling, a grandchild was falling down and crying, or one of His many disciples would drop by to ask Him a question or to massage His feet.

The other thing that Adele told me she found difficult to accept or to understand was His preoccupation with mundane details. He spent hours discussing with His wife or with one of His daughters the method of cooking, say, a summer squash: whether to boil it first or fry it directly in oil with some onions, spices, garlic. Still another subject of constant and interminable discussion was travel: Should He take the train to Bombay, or should He let His son-in-law, Ramji, drive Him in the neighbor's car? And, if so, at what time? It was far cooler to drive in the late afternoon, but this would mean that they would have to spend the night somewhere on the road, in a hotel, which would cost more, while if they left early enough in the morning, they could arrive in Bombay the same evening—Ramji was a reliable and experienced driver—providing that nothing went wrong with the car, an old Buick—a puncture, the motor overheating, an accident, all real hazards to be considered. In the train, on the other hand, instead of spending the night on the road at a hotel, He would have to buy a ticket for a berth in a sleeping compartment—at best, in a second-class compartment. But the train could be late, the train could be dirty, overcrowded, the sleeping compartments might already be sold out. Train travel, too, was full of unexpected dangers, to say nothing of the recent rash of bombings where whole trainloads of innocent people had been maimed and killed—and so on and so forth.

On the simplest expeditions, too—a trip to a neighboring village to buy fresh mangoes, a visit to the appliance store to look at a new electric fan—they would either arrive too early and no one was there yet, or they would be so late the store had closed for the day. One time, He had kept Adele waiting so long on a busy street corner that dozens of children had collected and surrounded her, touching her dress, her bare arms, her purse, and it had taken all her self-control, she said, not to burst into tears of rage and shame.

The same, Adele said, was true when he had spoken Hindi for an entire afternoon and Adele was the only person in the room who did not understand a word of what He was saying.

With Him, Adele told me there, at the Caribbean resort, she had to learn that nothing in India— no, not even the weather; wasn't it always hot, hotter, hotter still?—went according to plan.

Fifteen

Of the two children, Harry was the spitting image of Adele, while Nina took after Howard. Nina had Howard's fair complexion, his blue eyes, his fine blond hair. Nina often told me how she wished it had been the reverse and that she had been the one to inherit Adele's curly hair, Adele's olive skin which allowed Adele to tan easily—two days in the sun sufficed for Adele to get brown.

Adele, on the other hand, wished, she said, that she was more like her daughter, Nina. Nina was serious, Nina was dedicated, Nina was motivated. Nina, Adele liked to point out, was the one with the real talent in the family. Nina was the artistic one in the family.

Harry was the opposite, and the trouble with Harry, Howard said, was that Harry had no direction, no sense of purpose. And whenever Harry had gotten into trouble, someone—Adele usually—had always bailed him out. For instance, Howard would cite the time Harry was caught smoking pot, the time Harry drove the car without a valid license, the time Harry was put on probation in school for having a bottle of Scotch in his room.

Adele had continued to make up excuses. Some people were like that, Adele would tell Howard. Some people could not walk around the block or go to the corner without—through no fault of their own—getting into some kind of trouble. Harry could not help it, Adele said. Harry took after her.

Sixteen

Howard said how unfair it was. How others—he included himself, of course—had to pay the price. His affair with Melissa, for instance, not that it mattered, Howard was not in love with Melissa—the affair had just happened. Yes, he had been attracted to her. And yes, in a way, he could say he had the affair because he was angry. Who wouldn't be? But his affair with Melissa was nothing compared to

Adele's going off with that man. That guru. That char-
latan, whoever He was. The mere thought of Him,
even now, made Howard's blood boil.

Adele had left for months at a time. Adele had
not bothered to give Howard an excuse. Adele had not
bothered to explain to Howard. Adele had merely
picked up her small suitcase and walked out the door.
Irresponsible. Crazy. Nuts. If anyone else had done
this, he or she would go to jail. Or to the loony bin.
But not Adele. Adele got away with murder, Howard
said.

And Howard was not even going to get into the
business with the trainer, the horse trainer—what was
his name?—and how Adele had lied and said she was
in the city getting a haircut. And anyway, that had
nothing to do with what Howard and I were talking
about now—Howard and I were talking about the
dogs, or more precisely, the one remaining dog, Lily,
and how Howard, too, hoped to convince me.

Those poor dogs! Howard said. And what was he
to do? Here he was in his office all day with no one at
home and the cleaning woman had left the back door
unlatched so when the UPS truck had pulled into the
driveway, the three Irish setters had pushed the door
open and gone running out. They had stood around

the delivery truck barking, and the driver—he was new to the route, otherwise he would have known that the three big Irish setters were friendly—had been too frightened to get out of the truck and deliver the package. The Irish setters, too, must have sensed his fear because they barked louder at him. They had even jumped up against the truck, had scratched the door. In his hurry to leave, the driver had failed to look in both his rearview mirrors.

"No use blaming yourself," I told Howard. "You can't stay home all day. You have work to do."

In answer, Howard sighed and told me that of the three dogs, Heidi had been his favorite.

Seventeen

Adele said she was not religious, she was superstitious.
She believed in signs, in rituals. Already, she told me,
she had tried acupuncture, homeopathy, visualization,
various diets and regimens which included wheat grass
juice, Chinese roots and vegetables. To reach a
decision, Adele would toss a coin, swing her
pendulum, look up her sign in her chart, consult a
psychic, a palmist, a Tarot card reader, and finally,

one day a week, Tuesday, for nearly five years, Adele drove over a hundred miles round-trip in her car in order to talk about her dreams.

As an experiment, Adele described how she had once spent a whole day lying inside a tub filled with saline solution. Lying in the tub of saline solution was supposed to simulate and bring back the *in utero* experience. Notwithstanding that her skin ended up looking like a plucked chicken's, all goose bumps, Adele had a kind of revelation. The revelation, she claimed, was that she got to choose her own parents. Her father, even.

Adele was born two months premature and the Spanish nurse, the *aya,* Adele's mother had hired to look after her would soak Adele up to her neck in chicken soup.

The *aya*'s name was Carmen, and every day after school, when Adele was older, Adele used to go to church with Carmen. Carmen prayed and Adele knelt beside her. Sometimes, Adele and Carmen would kneel for an hour—Carmen's lips moving in prayer, her fingers fingering her beads.

The Christ on the cross in the back of the altar was life-size and must have been recently repainted— the colors were so vivid, so garish—and very often it would happen that after staring at Him for a while in the dim church, Adele would see the poor Christ's nailed hands and feet begin to twitch. Sometimes, too, Jesus Christ in His Torment would open His blue eyes wide at Adele, then squeeze them shut. His lips would part (Adele claimed she could see Christ's tongue) as if in an agonized shout: *Mira, mira, Adelita!* (Adelita was what the *aya* called Adele.) But the worst part was when Jesus Christ would shake His heavy head with its painful crown of thorns back and forth in said disapproval of her and His whole body would contort then, like the neighbor's dog who had epileptic seizures on the lawn.

Adele's legs got so stiff—like a cripple's, she said —that she had to lean both hands against the back of the pew to stand up. Afterwards, when she and Carmen stepped outside the church into the sunshine, the light was so bright Adele cried out.

Carmen was only four feet tall, a midget almost. But Carmen was strong. Sometimes, Adele would pretend to be tired or pretend to feel sick and make Carmen carry her home piggyback. Adele was nearly as tall as Carmen, and Adele could still remember how she would make herself a dead weight on Carmen's back—like a heavy cross Carmen had to bear—all arms and legs in poor Carmen's way.

Poor Carmen. If Adele had been religious, she would have believed that God would punish her for this.

Adele used to tease Carmen. Adele used to hide from her. When Carmen came to tell Adele it was time to get ready for school or it was time to eat supper, Adele would have disappeared from her room —Adele was not under the bed, Adele was not in the closet behind all the clothes, Adele was not locked in the lavatory.

Dónde? Dónde? Adele could hear Carmen screaming for her all over the house while, frantic, even the neighbor's dog would not stop his barking.

Eighteen

Around the time that Adele first met Him, Adele said she could not sleep. She would go to bed, she said, at a reasonable hour, at eleven or eleven-thirty, the time she and Howard usually went to bed at night unless they went out, and she would be yawning, she would be tired and ready to fall asleep—or so she thought—but the moment her head hit the pillow, she was wide awake again.

Adele was wide awake all night long. In bed, she tossed and turned, she could not find a position that was comfortable, while next to her, Howard fell asleep instantly and could sleep through anything. Adele tried taking hot baths, drinking glasses of warm milk, she read a book on money management (actually, the subject turned out to be quite interesting), she counted sheep.

One night by chance (although Adele said she did not believe in chance, she believed in *karma*), Adele had left the car keys in the ignition, and when, dressed in only her nightgown and robe, she went to the garage to get them, she decided to just drive around for a while—not far, she told herself. The first few nights, Adele drove in and out of the driveway, turned around on the main road, came back. After several nights, still wearing only her nightgown and robe, Adele became bolder. She drove into the village, past the local pharmacy, the hardware store, the new bakery, all of which were shut and looked different to Adele, smaller, shabbier, than they did in broad daylight. Then one night, she drove to the nearest town, past the station where Howard sometimes took the train, past her children's school, and to the shopping mall. In the shopping mall, there were a few cars parked at odd angles in a random fashion and Adele could not tell if the cars were abandoned, but she did not dare to stop, to look inside them and find out. After that night, Adele started to drive into the city. She drove into the city in a record short time—in a way, she wished she could have told Howard, who boasted that it only took him fifty minutes when really it took him over an hour—she drove down the wide deserted avenues. She experimented by taking different approaches to the city: the toll bridge, the Third Avenue Bridge, the two tunnels. One night, Adele found that she was driving past the city. Already she was in another state speeding south at eighty miles an hour and God knew how many miles away from home she was, from her sleeping husband, her sleeping children. She got frightened. At the same time, on the nearly deserted turnpike—except for the big trucks that somehow propelled Adele's car along with them by their weight, their mass—it required an enormous effort on her part to get off at an exit and turn back. It would have been much easier for Adele to have kept going—going, going, going—until, say, the car finally ran out of gas and forced her to stop.

Dressed in her cotton nightgown and robe, and in her bedroom slippers, Adele did not get home until seven o'clock that morning. Howard was already in the kitchen trying to fix the children their breakfast. For a moment, except that Harry and Nina were watching him, Adele thought Howard might hit her.

"Goddammit! Where in hell have you been?" Howard had said without looking at her.

Nineteen

According to the French boy who wore nothing but a bikini bathing suit and white sunscreen cream on his nose and who rented out the masks and the flippers and who took care of the boat so that the people staying at the resort could go water-skiing, the first time he saw Adele go swimming in the Caribbean, the three Irish setters, Heidi, Suzy, and Lily, as if those three Irish setters believed that they were fish—long-tailed, hairy red fish—had rushed into the ocean after Adele.

The French boy swore that Adele—Adele was swimming the crawl, face down in the water and only coming up for air every other stroke—had had no idea. (Adele was later to confirm what the French boy had said: the thought had never occurred to her. As far as Adele knew, the closest the three dogs had ever come to real water was the half-dried-up stream in the woods behind the house in Connecticut.)

After Adele had swum out a certain distance—*au moins un ou deux kilomètres*—Adele, the French boy said, had paused to lie on her back in the water, to catch her breath, to perhaps look at and admire the cloudless blue sky overhead. By then, too, the French boy was watching Adele through a pair of binoculars —*Adele est si belle*—and he saw, he said, the three Irish setters, Heidi, Suzy, and Lily, catch up to Adele.

The French boy said he could very well imagine how Adele must have felt—*Mon Dieu! Une peur bleue!* —when she heard those three Irish setters swimming toward her. Already, she must have pictured herself, first one leg—*une jambe, puis un bras*—then the other, and the water churning with her blood—*l'eau devenue toute rouge*—attracting other sharks, the way the

French boy told me he had, in fact, seen happen once. Only it had been a native boy—*le pauvre garçon*. The native boy—*le pauvre garçon*—was fortunate, he did not die. *Le pauvre garçon* had lost a leg and part of his arm.

Had he not been so absorbed watching Adele, the French boy swore that he would have gotten into his boat and gone right out to her—*à toute vitesse!* Instead, he kept looking as, way out there in the middle of the Caribbean, the three Irish setters—*ces trois gros chiens rouges*—tried to jump on Adele, tried to lick her face. The three Irish setters, Heidi, Suzy, and Lily, in their excitement at having caught up with Adele, the French boy said to me—*Mon Dieu, je vous jure que de toute ma vie je n'ai jamais vu quelque chose de semblable*—had damned near drowned Adele!

Twenty

What a pity! people—people I have never even met,
people I don't even know—come up to me still and
say.

> *You met her! You knew her! Adele was so good-looking.
> Not beautiful in a classical sense, but a handsome woman.
> An unusual woman. She had charm, she had energy. She
> could do anything. Didn't she run a marathon once?* those
same people say to me.

And didn't she go off to India with someone? A man? I went to India for three days and that was plenty! And what about her children? Three children. No, two children and three dogs! What happened to those three dogs? one of those people always asks me.

I have Lily. The other dog, Heidi, was run over by the UPS truck. Suzy, the third dog, ran away or was kidnapped, I don't know, I always answer.

Twenty-One

The rose thrown by a friend hurts more than any stone.

—A TURKISH PROVERB

While Adele and I were sitting together on chaises longues on the patio of my bungalow (my bungalow had a patio that gave directly onto the beach facing the sea, while Adele's was situated further down on the beach and had a rooftop terrace), Adele told me how she was lucky to have a room to herself in India (perhaps Adele said this in answer to a remark I made about the blue and green cotton cushion material), and never mind, Adele had continued, that her room was smaller than her coat closet, smaller even than her shoe closet back home in Connecticut, and never mind, too, that the room was airless and that the room did not look out into the street but onto an alley and faced the blank wall of a building. At least she did not have to share the room with Gita, His unmarried daughter, or worse still, with His mother-in-law or His widowed sister-in-law (one of whom snored, she snored worse than Howard, Adele said she could hear her through the thin walls). Already it was bad enough that she had to share the bathroom with them, which meant that Adele had to get up very early in the morning, otherwise she had to wait for hours before she could use the toilet, wash her face, brush her teeth.

Adele went on to describe how she had to use the rusty hook on the door of the small room to hang up her three skirts. There was no bureau (nor was there room for one), so Adele kept the rest of her clothes—her T-shirts, her underwear, her socks—in her duffel bag, which she stored underneath the narrow iron bed. Next to the duffel bag, she neatly lined up her two pairs of shoes. Adele used the wooden chair by the bed as a night table, and on it she kept her toiletries, her books, her papers, her pens.

The only light in the room came from a single naked light bulb which hung from the ceiling. Adele had tied a long enough string to the cord so that she could turn the light on and off while lying on her bed by pulling the string with her toes. To make the room dark at night, Adele had fashioned a window shade from an old cotton scarf.

At the beginning, when Adele first arrived in India, she had tried putting up decorations on the walls of her little room—a photo of Harry and Nina when they were little holding her horse, Sylvia Plath, by the halter; a photo of the three Irish setters, Heidi, Suzy, and Lily, taken in the garden outside the house in Connecticut; a postcard of van Gogh's sunflowers; an old-fashioned scenic postcard of India—but He had told Adele to take everything down.

Adele, He said sternly, had read enough books, seen enough paintings and photos to last her a lifetime. Adele, He said, should abstain from naming things. For during the interval between seeing a dog (the dog, Adele said, was her own example—He had used something else) and naming it a dog, illumination might come to her.

"And did it?" I asked, turning in my chaise longue to look over at Adele.

Twenty-Two

Even though you tie a hundred knots,
the string remains one.

—JALALUDDIN RUMI

Adele once told Harry, her son, that her first mystical experience, which strictly speaking was not mystical, took place, in all places, at one of those intercollegiate athletic meets. Adele was sitting on a wooden bench with the other swimmers, waiting for her event and looking at a wrestling match. She did not like wrestling (she liked it even less later when Harry took up wrestling in school). She did not like the sound of groaning and grunting the wrestlers made, she did not like watching the wrestlers—she knew some of them, some of them were her friends—senselessly hurl each other on the mats in the hammerlock, the chicken wing, the half nelson, contorted positions whose names she could never remember. Above all, Adele always worried that someone would get hurt. But this one time—although each time Adele told this story, she could never describe her feeling accurately —she had felt as comfortable sitting up there on the wooden bench of the grandstand as if she had been sitting on a comfortable sofa in her own living room. In addition, Adele had felt an enormous sense of benevolence, a love almost, toward everyone around her —her father, her teachers, the students, some of whom she would soon have to compete against herself, whom she did not know or with whom she usually felt shy or inadequate or defensive. Instead, the sound of people shouting, cheering, even the groans of the wrestlers, had been like music to her ears, and most important, Adele had felt—for a while anyway and until she had to get ready, until she had to put on her bathing suit—a sense of peace, a sense of oneness with everyone and everything, including the sweating, groaning wrestlers. To this day, Adele claimed, she could not remember—even if her life depended on it —what happened afterwards: whether she won or lost her swimming match.

Twenty-Three

Sometimes, when she would swim far out in the Caribbean, Adele would make believe to herself that she was swimming across the Atlantic Ocean. From there, she would do the butterfly stroke through the Straits of Gibraltar, or, if she was not pressed for time (if Howard was not waiting for her to have lunch), she would first do a leisurely backstroke around the Cape of Good Hope before swimming back to the balmier Mediterranean, where she would lazily float on her back for a while and look at the expensive yachts, the big white villas that dotted the shore, the fancy hotels on Cap Ferrat, Cap d'Antibes (where over forty years ago, Adele told me, her parents had spent their honeymoon); then turning over, Adele would follow the big tankers through the Suez Canal down to the Red Sea and to the too warm, oily waters of the Gulf of Aden, to the Arabian Sea which became the Indian Ocean (in the Indian Ocean, Adele had to keep a sharp eye out for the steamers and freighters that sailed dangerously close to shore), and to the Bay of Bengal, where she had to swim the crawl as fast as she knew how, to get past the shark-infested waters of the Andaman Sea down the Strait of Malacca, to the Bay of Siam, where, at last, she could stop to catch her breath for a moment on the white sandy beaches of Ko Samui, before plunging on again to the South China Sea, past the schools of flying fish to the Sea of Japan, where, again, she might pause an instant to dive for pearls underwater, before tackling the long journey back doing the sidestroke across the Pacific Ocean. If she still had the time (if Howard was not pacing up and down on the beach looking for her), Adele might detour and breaststroke around

Australia, New Zealand, Tasmania; she would swim along the warm equator, and stop off in Samoa, once more in the Galapagos, before giving one big scissor kick to cross the Panama Canal to swim back here to the Caribbean.

Twenty-Four

Rather than words comes the thought of high windows;
The sun-comprehending glass,
And beyond it, the deep blue air, that shows
Nothing, and is nowhere, and is endless.

— PHILIP LARKIN

Adele met Him in Chartres Cathedral. She met Him
while she was touring the châteaux of the Loire Valley
with Howard, Harry, and Nina. Coincidentally
(although, according to Adele, there are no such
things as coincidences, coincidences are miracles),
this was the day a piece of the Virgin Mary's tunic,
the *sacra camisa,* which is usually locked up in a
reliquary, is brought out, aired, and washed. There

is a large procession of all the townspeople of Chartres through the streets, and elaborate floats are built in honor of the *sacra camisa,* which also means that all the traffic is stopped.

In the rented VW bus, Howard kept saying things like: "Why of all days did we have to pick this damn day to visit Chartres?" In the back seat Nina and Harry were arguing with each other. To make matters worse, it started to drizzle. Adele remembered that the people walking in the procession had put up their umbrellas. It was impossible to find a parking place and they had had to leave the rented VW bus in a garage, which made Howard grumble again. They then had had to walk to the cathedral.

Once inside, Adele, too, was disappointed. Without the sun shining through the glass, the rose window was dark, dingy, not luminous like the pictures she had seen. Also, the cathedral was full of camera equipment, lights, transformers, large cables lay on the floor—Adele had to keep looking down at her feet instead of at the stained glass so as not to trip —and television crewmen were noisily packing up their stuff. The mass celebrated earlier for the sacred relic of the Virgin's tunic had been televised for *Antenne 2*.

Adele had gone to sit by herself in a pew and Howard said he would take Harry and Nina to a café across the square and wait for her there. Adele had already said that she was not religious but that she believed in signs, and sitting by herself in Chartres Cathedral in France that summer, Adele said she closed her eyes and prayed for a sign that would tell her what to do next about her marriage to Howard so that she would not have to decide. Adele did not like making decisions. In fact, Adele often changed her mind.

After a little while, Adele opened her eyes. The television crew had left and the cathedral was almost empty except for the few people scattered around kneeling in the pews and the man sitting next to her.

The man was Indian—an India Indian.

The Indian man had a beard and was dressed in a flimsy white pajama, a *dhoti*.

At first, Adele thought the Indian man with the beard might do something untoward—expose Himself to her. Or He might ask her for something—for money.

''Do you know what Napoleon said when he first visited Chartres?—'An atheist would be uneasy here.' ''

The Indian man spoke to her as if He knew her already, as if they had been speaking to each other for a long time.

"What?" Adele had to ask Him to repeat Himself.

" 'An atheist would be uneasy here,' is what Napoleon is supposed to have said when he saw Chartres Cathedral for the first time."

"Oh, Napoleon," Adele said. She could feel her face turning red.

Now, the Indian man was smiling at her. His smile was the sweetest, the most radiant, the most loving smile Adele had ever seen or could ever imagine. A smile that right away filled her with happiness —how could she describe this?—a smile that for some reason made Adele think of her father. The Indian man did not look at all like Adele's father. The Indian man was the very opposite of how Adele's father had looked. Adele's father had been tall, fair-skinned, clean-shaven, a distinguished-looking man who always wore a three-piece suit and who rarely smiled at Adele or at anyone.

The other thing that Adele noticed was the Indian man's eyes. His eyes were so bright and unblinking that Adele hardly dared look at Him. To her, His eyes were like tall windows that looked out onto empty spaces, and they gave her vertigo. His look, too, seemed to look right through her. She felt as if she were in the presence of a person with a special power, a person who could read her mind.

Adele did not know how long she sat there with Him—an hour? fifteen minutes? a few seconds? What she remembered was looking at the stained-glass window across from where she was sitting—*Notre-Dame-de-la-Belle Verrière,* Our Lady of the Beautiful Window (Adele said she learned the name later)—and the more she looked, the more the colors of the stained glass seemed to oscillate, to shift and change. From yellow, the Virgin Mary's dress had turned into a dazzling indigo; above her the white dove, all of a sudden, looked like a turquoise parrot. In another window, Charlemagne shone out cobalt, in a third window, Roland had turned azure, in yet a fourth, the Good Samaritan was lapis, while Saint Anne and the Furriers were a deep violet color. The entire vast interior of the cathedral had taken on a blue-green hue, an underwater look; in addition, a marbleized pattern like that of an aquamarine sea had settled on the arches, on the pillars, on the clerestory walls, on the carved figures of the choir, on the embroidered altar cloth, on, as far as Adele knew, the *sacra camisa,* too.

When Adele glanced down at her skirt, which was a beige linen, the skirt had turned navy. Her matching blouse was cerulean, the diamond on the fourth finger of her left hand was a sparkling sapphire.

Blue, blue, blue. The blue of the Caribbean. Blue was light, blue was love—Adele told me how she only understood this afterwards—it was so simple, so perfect. For a brief moment, Adele and Chartres Cathedral were one.

Then Adele had started to hiccup. Of course, she could not stay, she had to leave right away. Around her, people had looked up from their prayers, they were frowning at her.

Outside, it was still raining, and Adele found Howard, Harry, and Nina waiting for her in a café just as they had said they would, but nothing was ever again the same for her.

Twenty-Five

After Adele told me how she had met Him and after
she left to go back to her own bungalow further down
on the beach (or perhaps, since the sky was bright
with stars, Adele decided to go for a swim, although
the French boy who rented out the masks and the
flippers had warned Adele that at night the sharks
swam closer to the beach), I could not sleep.

I tossed and turned on my bed—I blamed the white wine I had drunk; Adele had only drunk mineral water—then I began to feel hot, hotter, hotter still, and I threw off all the covers from my bed and turned on the ceiling fan as fast as it would go. A few minutes later, however, I felt cold, freezing cold, in my whole life I had never felt so cold, and I turned off the ceiling fan, put on a sweater over my nightgown, found an extra blanket, and since that did not suffice, I heaped all the clothes I could find on top of my bed in an effort to warm myself. All night long, or so it seemed to me, it continued like this—first I was freezing cold, then I was boiling hot—until, at last, just before dawn I must have dozed off for a few hours.

In the morning when I woke up, the sun was shining brightly through the wooden window slats, and my legs, my arms, my back, especially my back, were a painful red from too much sun. Also, the more I thought about what Adele had told me the night before, the more I convinced myself that it was nothing but a dream—a fever dream: the Indian man, Napoleon, Chartres Cathedral.

The next time I woke up, it took me a moment to realize that the sound I was hearing—Adele's voice calling to the three Irish setters on the beach: "Here, Heidi, Suzy! Here, Lily!"—was not part of the same dream.

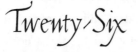

Twenty-Six

That day, Adele's three dogs, Heidi, Suzy, and Lily, did not recognize me. They barked at me. I wore sunscreen and a hat down to the beach.

When I showed Adele my burnt arms, my legs, my burnt back especially, Adele said the same thing had happened to Howard the last time, only Howard's sunburn had been much worse. Howard had had to stay in bed for two whole days.

"Thank God Howard stayed in Connecticut this time," Adele also said. "Thank God I persuaded Howard to send down the three dogs instead."

Adele was wearing the same red two-piece bathing suit, only she had put on a T-shirt over it—the T-shirt said *Horace's Lumberyard in Augusta, Maine.* She was patting one of the three Irish setters who had lain down next to her chair. (I think it was Heidi, although it could have been Lily—by then, I was pretty sure that I could recognize Suzy. Not only was Suzy the smallest of Adele's three dogs, she was the friendliest. Suzy was the dog who would come up to be patted, who would rub her head—almost like a cat—against my knee. Another thing I had remarked about Suzy was how, instead of lying flat like the other one did, her left ear would often flap open and expose the yellowish-pink inside part.)

"The dogs were another thing I could never get used to in India. I mean the way they are mistreated," Adele had continued. "How dogs are thought to be unclean. In front of His house, for instance, at any time of day or night, but especially at night, there are always packs of stray dogs roaming around in the streets, scavenging for food, for garbage, for anything to eat. And I've watched His little grandson—it's a game he plays—stand at the garden gate and throw stones at them. No one, not even his mother tries to stop him. And those poor dogs, you should see them, they are nothing but skin and bones, they are covered with sores, with fleas. Also, you should hear them. Some nights, they bark and bark, they never stop once. A few times I have tried to bring those dogs leftover food, leftover rice. One time I tried to pat one of those dogs, but those dogs have turned mean.''

"Here, Suzy," I called. "Suzy, come over here to me.''

Twenty-Seven

Seek knowledge, even as far as China.

— A SUFI SAYING

The second time Adele went to see Him, He looked quite different. He looked gray, old, thin. He had shaved off His beard. Adele thought He must be ill. Instead of asking her in, He made Adele sit outside His room on the floor of the corridor of the hotel in Bombay.

From Chartres, Adele had followed Him there. She had left Howard, Harry, and Nina driving in the rain in the VW bus and taken a plane. She told Howard she could not explain. She just *had* to, Adele said. There was no rational explanation. It was a feeling she had. Call the feeling an intuition. Call it an instinct, call it anything. Adele said that Howard would not understand anyway.

No one would.

Everyone who had walked past Adele—the waiters, the chambermaids, the other guests staying at the hotel in Bombay—had asked Adele what she was doing there, what she was waiting for. Adele could not answer them. By midday, Adele got so hungry that she ate part of a roll with marmalade on it from a leftover breakfast tray that was lying on the floor next to her in the corridor.

When, finally, He came out of His room, He frowned at her—Adele was sitting with her legs outstretched trying to shake circulation back into them. He told Adele that she had to leave now, but she should come back the next day.

The next day, Adele brought a newspaper, several magazines, a paper cup full of coffee, a roll to eat. No sooner had she settled herself down on the floor in the corridor outside His room and she was sipping the coffee, flipping through the pages of a magazine, than

He opened the door and told Adele to get rid of the food, to get rid of the reading material. Adele, He said, could neither eat nor read while she sat there, she was to move as little as possible, only if she absolutely had to. Adele, He said harshly, had to learn to stay quiet. Adele had to learn to do nothing.

For almost a week then, in Bombay, India—Adele's first trip East, and except during the taxi ride from the airport, all she got to see on that trip was the wall of the hotel corridor opposite her—Adele sat on the floor with her back straight, her legs crossed, her hands, palms up, resting lightly on her knees, and stared straight ahead of her.

Adele had to concentrate. Adele had to concentrate much harder than when she used to race in swimming meets, much harder than when she tried to learn to speak French (actually, Adele said, she had not concentrated at all then), much harder than when she got married to Howard and had to listen to what the investment adviser had said to her, much harder than when she was in labor and had to push out the two babies.

If, for only a moment, Adele let her mind wander, if, for only a moment, for instance, Adele thought about Howard, Harry, and Nina, and where they had gotten to in the rented VW bus—to the old walled city of Carcassonne? to a village perched on the side of a gorge in the Dordogne?—she would start to gasp, to struggle for breath.

Likewise, each movement Adele made, however small, however involuntary—licking the corner of her dry lips, wriggling her toes inside her sneakers—took up too much of her attention, too much of her energy, and again, Adele said, she would feel the way she did if she dove down too deep or too long in the ocean, her lungs ready to burst with insufficient air.

In, out, in, out—Adele tried to concentrate only on her breathing, on breathing as evenly as possible, on breathing as deeply as possible. Otherwise, if she did not, if she forgot, she was afraid, deadly afraid, she said, that the breathing would stop.

Meanwhile, the people—the waiters, the chambermaids, the other guests staying at the hotel in Bombay—who walked past Adele no longer bothered her. They no longer stopped or asked Adele what she was doing there. Stepping past Adele, they looked the other way. They made believe Adele was not there.

Twenty-Eight

"I know. I know. These things happen. My fault, as well," was what Howard said after Adele got back from Bombay.

Howard had then tried another tactic: "Adele, please tell me what it is that you want. A new car? An Audi 5000? What color—red? black?"

Howard had also tried to argue with her: "Adele, all those Indian swamis are alike. All they want is your money."

In the plane, on the way back from France, Adele kept writing and writing something down. Occasionally, she would look out of the window at the sky, at the clouds, sigh, and start writing again. In her neat rounded script, she wrote page after page in the bright orange pad on her lap—instead of lines, the pages had little squares like construction paper. At the top of each page, underlined, Adele wrote down a number: *1, 2, 3, 4, 5, 6*—she got up to *37*. While she was writing, Adele never once looked over at Howard —not even when they flew through such heavy turbulence that they had to keep their seat belts tightly fastened and the stewardesses temporarily halted the food and beverage service to go sit and strap themselves down as well.

In the seat behind Adele and Howard, Nina had leaned forward to ask: "From where I am sitting, it looks as if the wings are going to drop off, the plane is shaking so hard. Can that happen, do you know?" And Harry, in the seat next to her, had said: "This is what they mean when they talk about metal fatigue,'' to which Nina had replied: ''Mental fatigue? I was talking about the plane falling apart—not me, stupid!''

''Oh, shit! Do you sleep with him? Is that it?'' Howard had asked Adele in the end.

Twenty-Nine

Coincidentally—although I did not tell Adele this—I, too, had an Indian teacher. My yoga teacher, Mahesh. Mahesh had long thin arms and long thin legs and a disproportionately large chest from holding in and letting out his breath. Mahesh wore black wool shorts—the kind of scratchy black wool, I imagine, men wore in the forties—and wordlessly, Mahesh would contort himself into the *fish* (on his back, his legs crossed, his feet pressed to his thighs), into the *frog* (on his stomach, his legs bent back up, his feet at his sides, his hands pointing front—if it had not been for my sunburn, I could have shown Adele how), or, more difficult still, into the *pigeon* (in a back bend, on his knees and his elbows, his feet in his hands—a position I never learned to do correctly).

In his accented voice Mahesh told me how standing on one's head stimulated the brain cells, was the cure for fatigue, insomnia, idleness, depression, premenstrual tension—whatever ailed one. And I will never forget how one time while I was, in fact, standing on my head and I opened my eyes to look up at Mahesh—in his scratchy black wool shorts, Mahesh was standing next to me, he was holding on to my legs to steady me—I could not help but notice that Mahesh had an erection.

Thirty

The Master has no possessions.
The more he does for others,
the happier he is.
The more he gives to others,
the wealthier he is.

— TAO TE CHING

To Him, Adele traveled light. She traveled with only a carry-on, a small black duffel bag. She packed judiciously. Nina, her daughter, had seen her. Her mother, Nina said, packed two pairs of shoes—a pair of brown walking shoes, a pair of black sandals—four pairs of socks, four white cotton underpants (Adele had the narrow chest of a child—the only time she wore a bra, she said, was when she was pregnant), three print skirts, one black sweater, and four T-shirts.

The T-shirts were the problem. Adele could never decide. Adele told Nina how she had to pack the T-shirt she wore the time she ran the New York Marathon in under four hours—even if the T-shirt was getting worn out, the T-shirt, for her, was a talisman. She also had to pack the V-necked navy blue T-shirt with a picture of a turtle on it that Harry had brought her back from the year he spent in the Okavango Delta, and she had to pack the black sleeveless T-shirt she had bought from the one-legged street vendor in Madras who spoke Spanish and with whom she had the most amazing conversation and who Adele swore was enlightened, although probably he did not realize it.

"And black goes with everything, not that that matters," Adele told Nina, her daughter.

Adele also said that she could not decide between a gray T-shirt that said *Horace's Lumberyard in Augusta, Maine* on it and a white T-shirt that had a red Chinese character on one side and a blue Chinese character on the other side.

"Toss a coin, why don't you," Nina told her mother. "Heads, it's *Horace's Lumberyard in Augusta, Maine,* tails, it's the other T-shirt."

When tails came up, Adele said how the Horace's Lumberyard T-shirt fit her better, and how it was the one she was going to take with her anyway.

Nina said, "Can I have the other one, then—the one with the Chinese characters? What do the Chinese characters stand for, do you know, Mom? Peace? Happiness? Prosperity?"

"*Wendy's* is on the front, *Kentucky Fried Chicken* is on the back—just kidding, sweetie," Adele said to Nina.

Thirty-One

The first sin Adele ever committed was lying, stealing, and biting her *aya* Carmen's hand so hard she drew blood. (Adele had to make a list of all her sins for Him, sins from as far back as she could remember.) Adele bit Carmen when she was five or six years old, during that time when she and Carmen would stop off on the way home from school at a church to pray. Afterwards, Adele said, they would go to a store next door to the church that sold religious artifacts—Carmen was friendly with the salesgirl there. While Carmen and the salesgirl talked, Adele would browse in the store. Adele would finger the different kinds of rosary beads, she would inspect the plaster statues of the Virgin Mary and try to decide for herself which Virgin Mary she liked best, which Virgin Mary wore the prettiest dress, which had the kindest expression, until the day Adele noticed the beautiful little baby Jesus. The baby Jesus was made out of marble and was valuable—He was lying under a glass case on a velvet pillow. When Adele approached the glass case, the salesgirl, as if the salesgirl already knew what Adele was going to do before Adele herself knew, had suddenly looked up from her conversation with Carmen and had told Adele please not to touch.

From that day on, Adele became obsessed. Adele though about nothing else. At home, Adele prepared for Him. In her room, she built a crèche, she lined it with cotton, with scraps of material; for decoration, she lopped off the heads of her mother's red geraniums.

Once Adele had begun to remember her sins, she could not stop. Her list filled thirty-seven closely written pages beginning with biting her *aya,* Carmen, then lying to her mother about the red geraniums, all the way to lying to her mother about the boy, Paul, who was in the room with her (when Adele's mother had called out: *Adele, are you in there?* Adele had answered: *Only the radio!* when, in fact, on the bed, Paul had just come pressed up against her in his pants).

Besides lying to her mother, then lying to her father—how many times had she stolen his bottle of gin?—there was lying to Howard: lying to Howard about having an orgasm, lying to Howard about the cost of feeding and keeping a horse, lying to Howard about having an orgasm, lying to Howard about how it was cruel to own only one dog and not two (three was even better), lying to Howard about having an orgasm, lying to Howard about the affair with the horse trainer, lying to Howard about why she was out driving all night, lying to Howard about the best haircut she ever got in her whole life in Bangkok . . .

As for the baby Jesus, the glass case had been left unlocked, and while the salesgirl and Carmen were talking with their backs to her, Adele could not resist. Adele just reached in and took Him. She put Him inside the pocket of her school uniform. The next day, after Carmen had discovered the baby Jesus in Adele's room, Adele had had to go return Him to the store.

Red-eyed and with an elaborate bandage wrapped around her hand, Carmen had gone with her.

Por qué la mordió? the salesgirl had wanted to know.

When Adele would not answer her, the salesgirl told Carmen that Adele was no better than a *perro!*

Thirty-Two

Once there was a heart
and a thousand different thoughts;
Now there is naught
but La ilaha illa'llah.

—SHAIKH MAJDODDIN BAGHDADI

Women, women, women!

He was surrounded by women: His wife, His wife's mother (His mother-in-law), His brother's widow (His sister-in-law), His two daughters, Sonia and Gita, His two little granddaughters, and now her, Adele.

Adele, on the other hand, had had to leave her husband, her son, her daughter, her three dogs, Heidi,

Suzy, and Lily, Sylvia Plath, her horse, her relatives, her friends. Adele had had to give up all her possessions: her house, her furniture, her books, her pictures, her artwork, her clothes, her jewelry—He had even told Adele to take off the plain gold chain she had worn around her neck ever since she was fifteen years old that her first boyfriend, a boy named Paul, had given her. For according to Him, to possess anything is to be possessed by it.

In return, He had not—as Howard had accused Him of doing—promised Adele anything. He had not cast a spell on Adele. A spell, He said, would have been too easy, too simple. A spell would only prove that His will was stronger than Adele's, and this was mesmerism. There was nothing spiritual or difficult about mesmerism. On the contrary, when He was a young man, He claimed He deliberately refused to learn a mantra to cure epilepsy because for the rest of His life He would then have been obliged to render this service to all the people who would still be lining up right this moment outside His door. There were plenty of other people in India who could cure epilepsy, who could do snake bites, He said.

The reason, for instance, that He had made Adele sit all day for a week on the floor of the corridor outside His hotel room in Bombay, and everyone walking past had asked Adele what she was sitting there for, was so that Adele could forget everything she had ever learned. Adele, He said, had to empty out her mind of everything she had ever known.

Already, when she was with Him, Adele admitted, her mind slowed down, became almost blank. Adele could no longer think properly. If He sent her out on an errand, Adele had to concentrate hard to remember. It would happen that when Adele arrived at the market she had forgotten what she was supposed to buy. Soap? Rice? A new mat?

First, He said, Adele had to learn to control her breathing. She had to count each breath and in one breath she had to say *La ilah illa Allah* three times on the way in, and three times again on the way out. Eventually, in a single breath, He said, Adele would be able to repeat *La ilah illa Allah* nine times, then eighteen times.

He could hold His breath for twenty minutes. He shut His eyes and became very pale, very silvery, nearly transparent-looking—Adele swore that she had seen Him do this. Sitting cross-legged on a grass mat on the wood floor, Adele said, He could just as well have been carved out of stone, carved out of metal, and however hard Adele stared at Him, Adele could not see a single sign that He was alive: a pulse, a blink of an eyelash, a twitch of a muscle. (Again, nothing, *nada*.) And twenty minutes was a long time. Adele got frightened. She felt the way she might feel on a plane —Adele had tried to explain, and she was not one of those people who are afraid—that was going down— *down down down*—and that was taking too long to reach the ground and crash.

When He had finished, He let out a small breath, a small cleansing breath—*Hi*. Then, as if nothing special had happened, He started to laugh—swear to God, Adele had said—and He told Adele that if Adele really wanted to see something special, if Adele really wanted to be impressed, Adele should have seen Him do this thirty years ago when He was a young man. Before He got married, before He had sex, He could hold His breath, He said, for twice as long. For an hour. For an hour and a half.

Or, He said, Adele could go and take a look at the holy people by the Ganges River who could separate from their limbs, who could leave their arms, their legs, their heads. Only men could do this. Women, He said, could do other things. Women, He told Adele, could walk on water.

Thirty-Three

Deep in the sea are riches beyond compare.
But if you seek safety, it is on the shore.

— S A A D I

Another thing I remember about the restaurant high up on the cliff at the Caribbean resort is not just how the people were remarking on Adele's swimming so far out to sea, but how the waiters became so engrossed watching Adele that they forgot to take down people's orders, they forgot to serve people their food. A number of people had started to complain:

Waiter! Waiter! I've been waiting twenty minutes!

Waiter, where is the dessert I ordered? The tirami su?

The waiters, every chance they got, went to stand against the railing of the restaurant terrace with their backs to the people who were eating lunch and they watched Adele and the three Irish setters swim further and further out in the ocean.

"She must have been an Olympic champion once," guessed the waiter standing nearest to me.

"Maybe she swam the English Channel," observed another waiter who was leaning against the railing next to him.

"She's a guest at this hotel. She comes nearly every year," said a third waiter. "I've seen her. She and her husband—come to think of it, I haven't seen her husband this year. They always sit at the same table, the table over there, the table close to the sea. And she does not eat meat. She does not eat fish. She's a vegetarian."

"Ha ha! No wonder!" said the first waiter. "The fish are going to eat *her*! Her and her three dogs!"

Thirty-Four

*Lalla Mimunah in the Magreb, a poor negro woman,
asked the captain of the boat to teach her the ritual
prayer, but she could not remember the formula correctly.
To learn it once more, she ran behind the departing boat,
walking on the water. Her only prayer was: "Mimunah
knows God, and God knows Mimunah."*

— A SUFI LEGEND

In India, Adele said, she even had to give up swimming
—swimming in the Indian Ocean which she could see
from the hotel in Madras where He had taken Adele
and His whole family on a holiday, and from where,
every morning, she would walk down to the beach
with Him (the sand there was dark, coarse, and not
like the sand here in the Caribbean). During that time,
Adele also said, she had never seen Him so cheerful,

so receptive, so accessible (He looked a lot younger, boyish, rounder almost, as if all of a sudden He had gained fifteen pounds).

Adele had wanted to take advantage of His good humor (and for once, too, she had Him to herself), she had wanted to ask Him a lot of questions: *Does love begin where the mind stops?* or, *Does man have a fixed nature?* or again, *Is there a unity of consciousness?*

Instead, she found that in spite of herself, in spite of all her efforts, she could only talk to Him about the most trivial matters, about the most mundane subjects, as if her vocal cords, her tongue, her lips, had lives of their own over which Adele had no control. On their walks down to the beach, for instance—it made Adele blush to remember this—she could do nothing but complain to Him about the hotel's lack of sanitary accommodations: the single bathroom, the lack of hot water, the lack of water, period. Adele said she could not help herself, she could not stop herself from describing to Him how every time she went to use the bathroom, there was not enough water to take a shower, not enough water to wash, not enough to flush.

He, of course, had answered her by saying that she was too squeamish, too fastidious. Most Americans

He knew were. In India, right away they became ill. Instead, and this would be a good test for her, Adele, He said, should not take a bath or wash for a week— no, during the entire stay at the hotel, Adele, He said, should not even brush her teeth!

Habits create limitations, He told Adele. Limitations, in turn, create suffering. This was the reason why He never ate a meal or bathed at the same time of day. Some days, He told Adele, He took His shower in the mornings, some days in the evenings. Some days, He took several showers a day. Some days, He never showered at all.

Each day, too, as Adele grew progressively dirtier—never mind that she changed her skirt, put on a clean T-shirt, a fresh pair of underwear—she felt as if a thin, almost invisible layer of filth, like a carapace, was covering her skin. In addition, she smelled. She caught whiffs of the fishy odor that emanated from under her arms, from in between her legs, from everywhere she perspired. When she put her hand to her face and breathed into it, she could smell her sour mouth—the same smell as when one of her fillings had fallen out. Her curly hair hung in limp greasy strands around her face; Adele had to tie it back with a rubber band.

The more unclean Adele had felt, the more she had looked longingly out at the ocean, the Indian Ocean. The Indian Ocean, however, was gray, the water flat, oily-looking, polluted. Still, Adele had stuck one hand in, then the other, and since the beach that day seemed deserted, she became bolder, she went all the way in. A quick swim, she told herself, was not the same as a bath or a shower (after all, she would not use soap), or the same as washing herself. A quick swim, Adele told herself, would not be disobeying Him.

Adele got caught by the outgoing tide. The tide and the current combined were so strong that even Adele could not swim against them. Since Adele also knew enough not to waste her energy, she let the tide and the current carry her out past the spot where, in a neat pile on the beach, she had left all her clothes, until she could feel the great pull out to sea weaken and until she could finally swim in.

But it was not the swimming, and it was not the ocean, Adele was to keep repeating later (to Gita, to Sonia, even to Ramji, to whoever would listen)—she could have stayed out in the water much longer, the water was warm—but the indignity.

The boys playing volleyball on the beach had

dropped the ball to watch Adele swim in. When Adele was finally able to touch bottom with her feet and was emerging naked from the sea, the boys stood poised ready to run, and by the time Adele stepped onto the beach and was calling out to them, "Wait! Could you wait for me, please!" frightened by what they had seen, the boys had disappeared.

In the boys' place, no longer looking either boyish or cheerful, and appearing to hold or to have something in front of His chest which Adele did not immediately recognize—to her, at first, it looked like the boys' volleyball and not His breasts—He was standing there waiting for her.

Thirty-Five

Adele's other passion—besides swimming—was horses. Pictures of Man O' War, Citation, Native Dancer had covered her bedroom walls. Blue, red, yellow, and white horse show ribbons had dangled from her dresser. For years, Adele said how she used to spend the hours she did not have to spend swimming laps in the school pool at a nearby stable—currying horses, cleaning tack, mucking out stalls. In return, she got to ride John Milton. (Adele said the two women who owned the stable named all their horses after poets, and Adele would never forget, she said, how Emily Dickinson was the meanest of all the horses. If anyone went near the door to Emily Dickinson's stall, Emily Dickinson right away would lay back her ears, bare her big yellow teeth.)

The rest of the time Adele would make it up. *Click, click, click,* Adele would go with her tongue. *Giddyup,* she would kick the imaginary John Milton in between her legs into a high-stepping trot. *Whoa,* she would shout to him. *Whoa, I said. Easy, John. Easy there, boy.*

Adele had what you call a natural seat on a horse. She rode with her ass. Adele used muscles that most people don't even know they have. She said it came from riding bareback and from doing dressage—not on John Milton. Poor old John Milton—believe it or not—went blind. He had to be put down.

Adele had a way of sitting in the saddle that is hard to describe, a way of bearing down her weight from her shoulder blades to her tailbone. Adele rode a horse with her stomach sticking slightly out, the way only women with flat stomachs can. She held the reins loosely in one hand, her elbows at her sides. Even if the horse broke his stride, stumbled, or shied suddenly, her legs never budged. The balls of her feet always rested lightly in the stirrups. When it came time to dismount, Adele swung a leg in front of her over the pommel, the hard way, and jumped to the ground.

Mainly, Adele was not frightened, and a horse can tell. A horse can tell instantly by the voice, by the smell.

When Adele was married to Howard and they lived in Connecticut, Adele kept a horse in a field behind the house. The big gray mare she named Sylvia Plath (although by then the two women had long since gone and sold their stable). According to Adele, Sylvia Plath was such an extrovert she should have belonged to a circus. Not only did Sylvia Plath love to show off, but if ever she heard music, Sylvia Plath would prick up her ears, arch her neck, and with her long white tail swishing back and forth, do a kind of four-step jig.

One time, accidentally, Sylvia Plath put her foot in a gopher hole and fell. Adele went right over Sylvia Plath's head and came down so hard on her backside —or, perhaps, she came down on a log or a stone— the pain was so sharp Adele almost passed out. Afterwards, however, the strange thing was that Adele became—for a day or two, anyhow—prescient, clairvoy-ant.

When the phone rang, Adele knew that it was her mother-in-law calling long-distance from Chicago. Adele knew what kind and what color the cars on the road in front of her house were before they drove by and while they were still stopped on the corner at the stop sign. Adele knew that her son Harry's team had lost the wrestling match before Harry called to tell her and that her daughter, Nina, had gotten an A− on her algebra test even before Nina's math teacher, Miss Maxwell, had graded it. More important, Adele knew that the reason Howard, her husband, was late getting home from work every night that month was not the work as he had said to Adele it was, but a woman named Melissa.

In retrospect, Adele realized that the fall from the horse must have activated her *chakra kundalini*.

"Your chakra what?" I remember I asked Adele.

The same thing, Adele said she learned later, had happened to a woman who fell down her basement steps in Ontario, Canada. As a result of the fall, the woman could read people's minds.

"So, tell me, Adele—what am I thinking?" I said.

Thirty-Six

Lily is such an obedient and beautiful dog that everyone admires her. She has not been much trouble except for that one time in the park when I was talking to another dog walker—I don't remember what about, maybe something to do with the advantage of having two dogs instead of one, they keep each other company—and Lily ran off. One moment Lily was right there beside me playing with a dog who was part golden retriever, part Great Pyrenées, and the next moment when I looked down again, she was gone.

Lily took off so fast (especially since I have already said how Lily is no spring chicken, how Lily is twelve) she could have been part whippet, part greyhound. All I could see of Lily was her long feathery tail which she held straight out like a pennant as she went running after a horse who was trotting briskly down the bridle path. The dappled gray horse had a prancing circus horse gait and a way of tossing his head and swishing his tail which, probably, made him look a lot like Sylvia Plath, the horse Adele used to have, and from the back, I have to admit, the horse's rider too looked a lot like Adele. The rider was thin, the rider had a good seat, the rider was wearing a hard hat so that I could not see what her hair looked like, although I caught a fleeting glimpse of a few curly strands sticking out from under the brim.

"Lily!" I yelled. "Come back here!

"Lily, Lily!" I started to run after her down the bridle path.

I ran and ran (unlike Adele, although I exercise and I do yoga, I could never run a marathon, and at the time, I was wearing a skirt, stockings, high heels), until I was so out of breath I could no longer call out Lily's name. Instead, I had to stop, lean against a tree, rest for a bit.

For over an hour, I looked and looked for Lily. Only when it began to get dark did I start to walk back home with the empty leash still dangling from my hand. By then, I had convinced myself that Lily was gone, that I would never see Lily again, when all of a sudden, behind me, I heard the metal jingle of a choke collar with tags attached to it.

''Lily!'' I cried.

I started to speak sternly to her, to scold her, but I could tell by just one look at her shiny red coat which was matted with dirt, one look at her long legs which were shaking with fatigue, one look at her pink hanging-out tongue flecked with saliva, that it was pointless. Lily, I felt sure, knew as well as I did the mistake she had made.

Thirty-Seven

He who sleeps on the road will lose either his hat
or his head.

—NIZAMI

Another thing Adele complained about was how hard
it was for her to exercise in India, and walking to and
from the market every morning did not suffice. It was
too hot and the streets were too crowded, Adele could
not maintain any sort of stride. She always had to
dodge groups of young men loitering and smoking on
street corners who looked at her with suspicion—or
was it derision?—old women carrying large baskets or

heavy pails filled with sloshing water, children running past and bumping into her accidentally-on-purpose, not to mention that Adele had to keep a sharp eye out for beggars, for pickpockets—often, one and the same person.

The closest she had come, Adele said, to getting any form of exercise was playing a few games of Ping-Pong with Ramji, Sonia's husband. Adele had found the Ping-Pong table (along with a wheelbarrow that had no wheel and a rusty bicycle that had no handlebars) in a shed behind the house—the table was so battered and the green paint so chipped Adele had not recognized right away what it was. Also, the little net was badly torn—only one side of it was still held to the table with a clip, the other side just dangled down over the edge. On a dusty shelf in the shed, she had found two Ping-Pong rackets (the rubber covering equally worn off on each), and she had managed to buy Ping-Pong balls at the market (afterwards, His grandchildren had fought over and lost the balls). The only trouble was, Adele said, the first game she played she beat Ramji 21 to 6. Ramji had blamed his Ping-Pong racket, so that Adele had had to exchange her racket, which was no better, for his, and when, the next game, Adele still beat him easily—even more easily, Adele won 21 to 4—Ramji said it was not fair, he was out of practice; he refused to play with Adele again. Adele had then tried to teach Sonia and Gita, His two daughters, how to play Ping-Pong, but the two young women had giggled and hit the ball—their slender arms jingling with silver bracelets—so wildly into the air that the ball bounced off the walls and ceiling of the shed instead of off the Ping-Pong table, and Adele had given up.

"There's a Ping-Pong table here," I said to Adele. "I've seen it, it's where they keep the masks and the flippers. If you want to play."

Adele shook her head. Then, sitting up in her beach chair she changed her mind. "Yes. Okay, let's play a few games," she said.

As with Ramji, Adele beat me 21 to 6 the first game. The second game I did a little better, she only beat me 21 to 13. We were about to begin a third game when the French boy who rented out the masks and the flippers came in and said how he had once been the Ping-Pong champion of the village he was from, a village near Toulon, and he, too, wanted to play with Adele.

I stayed around for a while, long enough to watch Adele beat the French boy 21 to 14.

Thirty-Eight

Let the miracle be done, even though Mohammed do it.

—A SPANISH PROVERB

"He tells stories," was how Adele answered me another time while we were swimming in the Caribbean. "The stories are parables, allegories with layers of meanings. Hidden meanings. My favorite is the one about Abdul-Qadir of Jilan who after saying his prayers one day threw one of his wooden sandals up in the air, then the other. Neither sandal came back down to the ground. A few days later, a caravan was attacked by Arab bandits. The bandits killed most of the people, stole their horses, their camels, their merchandise. The people who survived the attack fell to their knees and prayed to Abdul-Qadir that they might still reach Baghdad in safety. As soon as they finished their prayers, they heard loud cries and they thought their attackers were returning to kill off the rest of them. Instead, the bandits came and begged them to accept back their property—the horses, the camels, the merchandise which they had stolen from them. A calamity had befallen the Arab bandits. The two leaders of the bandits were lying dead. A wooden sandal lay next to each leader's head.''

There was not a breath of wind that day. The sea was absolutely still and as flat as a tray except for where the water broke in small frothy waves along the shore. While Adele talked, I lay floating on my back in the transparent blue-green water. Occasionally, I made a paddling motion with my hands to keep afloat. In the distance, I could hear a motorboat.

''He says that miracles have to do with causation, and causation has to do with problems of time and space,'' next to me in the water, Adele continued, ''like Albert Einstein. The reason too, He says that the

Qadiri dervishes can walk on water, the reason the Azimia appear at different places at the same time.''

I looked at the cliff that rose straight up from the beach, the sides covered with red, orange, purple bougainvillea blossoms, with delicate sweet-smelling frangipani, with bright red hibiscus flowers that every day were cut fresh and placed in the vases at each table in the restaurant. I could also make out the striped green and white awning which protected the tables and the people eating at them from the hot sun and from the sudden tropical showers that usually lasted only a few cooling minutes.

''Who? Albert Einstein?'' I said as I turned over onto my stomach and started to swim back to shore, deliberately leaving Adele alone in the water.

''Wait,'' I heard her call out after me. ''I am just repeating what I have heard Him say—proof that things are not what they seem.''

In the restaurant, I would deliberately spill sugar on the tablecloth, a few inches from my coffee cup and plate, so that the little yellow birds—sugar birds, the waiters called them—would land at my table. Only that morning, a waiter had told me how he once saw a man—also a guest at the resort—catch a sugar bird with his bare hand. The bird had been busy eating the spilt sugar on the tablecloth, just as the birds at my table were doing (if I so much as bent a finger around a spoon the birds took fright and flew away). The man's hand, the waiter said—and he had watched him carefully—had moved quicker than the eye. The man must have been a magician, I volunteered. The waiter said no, he did not know. The man, the waiter said, was not from here.

Thirty-Nine

Have I said already how, to this day, Howard keeps a picture of Adele on his desk and how, in the picture, Adele is wearing running shorts, a T-shirt with the number 1855 pinned to it, a cap with the visor turned around backwards, how she has one of her arms raised up in the air, her two fingers spread in a V, and how she is grinning? Not even out of breath, Howard said to me, she could have continued, while the next woman after Adele to cross the finish line collapsed.

Again, Adele was lucky. The weather was perfect. Cool, Howard said he remembered, with a light breeze. At the start on the bridge in the early morning, it had been colder. Adele had worn sweatpants over her running shorts, a sweatshirt, and a nylon windbreaker. During the race, she had discarded these. She threw her clothes out to the crowd somewhere in Queens, and she saw someone pick up the sweatpants, the sweatshirt, the windbreaker—not just as a souvenir but, in that neighborhood, clothes someone would wear or sell.

Crossing the bridge was the only time Adele had admitted to feeling afraid. She was afraid that she would fall down, be trampled, there were so many runners. Right after the bridge, it was all right again, the runners fanned out.

At the beginning, Adele had run by herself in a loosely formed group made up mostly of women; at mile four, three Frenchmen caught up with her.

Alors? Ça va?

Gracias. Muy bien.

The Frenchmen wanted to know which restaurants Adele could recommend to them.

Adele had bought a book. She had trained for six months—not a day longer. Every morning, no matter what the weather was like, she got up at six and ran through the back roads of Connecticut. The reason Adele decided to run the marathon was that Howard bet her she couldn't. The longest distance she had run so far was eighteen miles, but according to her book, she should not worry. Adrenaline.

Adele would never forget, she afterwards told Howard, the people lined up along the streets cheering. Their noise filled her with happiness, it spurred her on. Never before in her whole life except for, perhaps, that one time during the wrestling match had Adele felt such a feeling of oneness, such a feeling of love for everyone.

Go 1855! Looking good! a woman holding a child in her arms had shouted to her from a blur of faces.

You can do it! a man stepping off the curb to hand Adele a paper cup full of water had yelled at her.

Adele never stopped—not even when she was taking off her clothes. (She jogged in place as she removed first one leg, then the other from her sweatpants.) After the Frenchmen had left her, Adele ran alone for a few miles; then she ran with a woman whose long blond hair was tied back in a braid. The woman was named Marina, and at the twenty-mile mark, Marina had to stop on account of a cramp. Before this happened, Adele and Marina had talked to each other as if they were long-lost friends meeting again. They had talked about everything—Marina had just broken up with her boyfriend, before that she had had an abortion—so that, completely absorbed, Adele had not even noticed when she finally crossed into Manhattan.

After the marathon, Adele had soaked in a hot bath. For the first time in months, she ate a steak— rare. Still too excited to sleep, Adele had insisted on going out to celebrate. At two o'clock in the morning, while Howard and her friends were yawning and complaining about how it was Sunday and how late it was getting, Adele was still on the dance floor.

Forty

I have a photograph of Adele and me taken on the
beach. I don't remember who took the photograph,
probably the French boy did. Adele has her arm
around my shoulder (one can just see her hand), and
we are both standing squarely in front of the camera.
As usual, Adele is wearing her red two-piece bathing
suit; I am wearing my one-piece blue bathing suit.
One can see how Adele and I are approximately the

same height (five feet eight and five feet seven and a half inches, respectively), how I probably weigh a few pounds more than Adele, and one can also see how Adele's hair is dark, except for a few white streaks in it, and how her hair is curlier and shorter than mine. (In fact, Adele's hair was so short, to me it looked shorn, although Adele swore to Howard that the best haircut she ever got in her whole life was in Bangkok, it was luck, no, it was *karma,* and Adele said this in such a way that Howard had asked her again what else she did in Bangkok besides getting her hair cut.) In addition, Adele's face is an oval shape while mine is rounder, her nose is long, straight, my nose turns up a little at the end, and finally, if one looks closely enough, since in the photograph we both have our sunglasses pushed up on top of our heads (and even though we may both be squinting a bit in the sun), one can still see how my eyes are brown while Adele's eyes, which in certain lights and at certain times of day looked so dark that they may have appeared brown, are in fact blue.

Blue.

The same blue as the Caribbean, the sea one can see in the photograph.

Forty-One

It was not easy. Adele said she had tried to resist Him.
In Connecticut, she had joined a book club
(unfortunately, the book club's selection for that
month was E. M. Forster's *A Passage to India*). She
had then tried oil painting, she had tried watercolors,
life-drawing classes. (Adele denied that she had any
talent for it—not like her daughter, Nina. Nina,

Adele said, had talent. Nina, Adele predicted, was going to go places with her art.)

Finally, one day a week, on Tuesday (the same day Adele drove into the city to talk about her dreams and to get her hair cut), dressed in her tailored navy blue suit and white silk blouse, Adele led groups through the museum. She would explain the effect, for example, of the Spanish Civil War on Picasso's paintings (she pronounced *Guernica* in the proper Spanish way), she would go on to describe how Cézanne wanted to capture the essence of color, how Mondrian rearranged space, and Adele talked so much that she began to loathe the sound of her own voice.

The day came—as long as she lived, Adele said, she would never forget this—when she stood in front of a painting and could not speak. Her mind went blank. Totally blank. She could not think of a single thing to say about the art, about the artist, not if her life had depended on it. All the people in her group had stood around and waited politely for Adele to begin. One woman coughed, another woman laughed nervously. Adele just stood there with her mouth wide open, but not a word, not a sound came out of it.

Nothing.

Nada.

Strangely enough, Adele told Nina, her daughter, later, the day this occurred coincided with the day the Francis Bacon show opened at the museum, and what, of course, struck Adele right away was Francis Bacon's obsession with people with *their* mouths wide open—life imitates art, Adele was to say to Nina—only instead of those people being incapable of speech the way Adele had been, the people in Francis Bacon's paintings were screaming.

Forty-Two

Adele and I were sitting together on the beach——on the third or perhaps it was on the fourth day, every day at the Caribbean resort was the same: cloudless, sunny, hot——a habit we had gotten into (only, now, I was careful, I wore a hat, a T-shirt, sunscreen); the three Irish setters, Heidi, Suzy, and Lily, were lying not far from us in the shade of the oleander bushes, and I was watching someone water-ski on one ski behind the motorboat driven by the French boy, and Adele who was also watching said how she could not look at anyone water-ski without feeling sick to her stomach.

As long as she lived, Adele said, she would never forget the summer when she was fifteen years old and she was water-skiing on Long Island Sound. Her father was driving the boat—her father, Adele was certain, had had a few drinks already—and Hasan, the big brown poodle Adele had grown up with, was in the boat, too. Hasan loved the water, he loved to swim, and actually, in the old days, Adele said, before they became lapdogs, poodles were retrievers who were sent into the freezing-cold water to fetch back ducks and to fetch back the shot fowl. In any case, Hasan was accustomed to going in the boat with them—unbidden he always leapt in, he always sat in the bow—and to this day, Adele was not sure what had happened. Only she remembered that she had yelled to her father to turn back and she had motioned to him with one arm that she was tired and that she had had enough, and the last thing she remembered, just as with her skis she started to cross back inside the boat's wake, was seeing Hasan stand up in his seat in the bow—maybe Hasan had gotten bitten by something, a bee or a horsefly, this happened sometimes, and he had stood up to snap at it—while Adele's father, to see what Adele was shouting about, had turned around. Adele's father had turned around in this awkward way, and to this day, Adele could see him move as if in slow motion, and not react fast enough, and Adele's father had turned his back on Hasan.

Adele screamed, she said. She screamed and screamed and screamed. She could not stop screaming even after she had let go of the rope and her skis had come off and were drifting away and she was treading water and water was going up her nose and water was getting in her mouth and she was coughing and spitting the water out, and still she kept on screaming and screaming as in the water right past her, so that she could have reached out and patted it, floated—no, bobbed like a goddamned red apple, Adele said— Hasan's severed head.

Forty-Three

Beat the dog and the lion will behave.

—A SECRET PHRASE USED
BY THE WHIRLING DERVISHES

Adele never went to Him empty-handed. She always
brought Him a gift. He would thank her politely;
then, very often, before He even opened the
package, before He even looked inside the box
to see what was in it, He gave away Adele's gift.

"Here, take this," He would say to the local
half-blind, half-mad beggar who stood all day by His
gate.

"But—" Adele would look away. She would try hard to fight back her tears. The alpaca sweater had been for Him. The beige V-necked sleeveless alpaca sweater—warm in winter, cool in summer—had cost her nearly three hundred dollars.

In a single day, His three grandchildren would have devoured the box of expensive Swiss chocolate Adele had brought Him. (During the long flight out, Adele had held the box carefully on her lap so that the chocolate would not get crushed.) Only a few half-eaten chocolates were left—the ones with the cherry liqueur fillings, the ones the three grandchildren had not liked and had put back in the box after taking a bite from.

Nor would He have stopped them.

"The chocolate is very rich. It will make the children sick," Adele would complain to Sonia, their mother.

Busy in the kitchen grating a coconut, Sonia shrugged her pretty, thin shoulders.

Sometimes He would ask Adele for a specific item:

"Next time you stop off in Hong Kong could you get me one of those pocket-sized solar-operated calculators."

Or, "If you see a pair of size 10 Nike running shoes with the cushioned heel, could you buy them for me."

Adele spent hours, days, weeks doing His bidding. For the Nike running shoes, she went to every sporting goods store in the Connecticut area, then in the city—the stores were out of stock on His size or else on the model He wanted. In the end, Adele had had to call the Nike distributor. The distributor sent Adele a printout with the telephone numbers of all the stores in the country that sold their products. Adele was lucky. After calling dozens of stores in the tristate area, Adele found a store in Albany, New York, that had a pair of the size 10 running shoes left, so did a department store in Trenton, New Jersey. To be certain, Adele ordered the running shoes from both. As luck—bad luck this time—would have it, the store in Albany, New York, sent Adele the wrong size running shoes, size 10^1/$_2$, while the department store in New Jersey sent two different shoes in the Nike shoe box: a Nike and a New Balance.

Howard, too, at the time, had joked—Adele had not left him yet—and Howard had also been dead serious, that he was going to hide all his good English shoes—Howard wore size 11, still how could he be certain?—from Adele. Howard's shoes, Howard's sports shirts, Howard's favorite terry-cloth robe, Howard's belts and suspenders—who knew, Howard said, what Adele might suddenly decide to bring to Him in India? Already Howard was missing the pair of pajamas Nina had given him for Christmas—elegant silk French pajamas—and Howard had accused, wrongly probably, the laundry of losing them.

As for the Nike running shoes—when finally Adele was able to locate the correct matching pair in size 10 and she had brought them to Him, He wore them once around the garden before He took them off and tossed first the one, then the other running shoe into the air and over the garden fence.

Forty-Four

But speaking of presents, one day when I forgot
to bring mine down to the beach, Adele lent
me the black T-shirt she said she had bought
from the one-legged street vendor in Madras who
spoke Spanish and who she said she was sure was
enlightened, the time she disobeyed Him by going
swimming in the sea. Later, when I tried to return

the black T-shirt to Adele, Adele shook her head.

"No, it fits you better anyway," she said.

"*Gracias,*" I said.

"*De nada,*" she said.

I wear the black T-shirt still.

Forty-Five

The worst part, according to Nina, was the money—
the money Adele was spending. Adele, Nina said,
spent money as if there were no tomorrow, or as if
money grew on trees, or as if money— But Nina was
not just speaking of the money that Adele spent to
travel with Him (airplane tickets back and forth to
India, train tickets for His whole family—how many
people? eight? nine? more maybe?—to and from

Madras, as well as the hotel accommodations, to say nothing of the expensive presents she bought for Him). Nina was speaking of the checks Adele was writing. Every day, Adele made out a new check to Him. Checks for a hundred dollars, checks for a hundred and fifty dollars, two hundred, sometimes five hundred dollars, a few checks made out—oh, it made Nina sick to even think of this!—to as much as a thousand dollars. And as Howard had warned Adele over and over again, Adele should not be spending her capital—hadn't Harry gone all the way out to India to try and convince her? Adele should be living off her income. Howard had even spoken to Adele's banker about this, but what could the poor man do when Adele would not listen to him. Where money matters were concerned Adele was stubborn, Adele would not listen to anyone. If what Howard said was true, who knew?—one day, Adele might cash a check for the whole damn thing. Whenever Nina brought up the subject of money, Adele, she said, would just sit there with that silly spiritual grin on her face and say: *But, sweetie—*

Forty-Six

How many times, I asked myself, from where I was sitting sunbathing on the beach, have I watched Adele churn the water with her arms—up down back up down back—as rhythmically and evenly as a paddle wheel, and kick up spray continuously with her feet, as she backstroked further and further from the shore with those three big Irish setter dogs swimming along with her? Or how often have I seen Adele, in a sudden burst of energy, spread her arms and beat an arc of water, her mouth open for air, her head and torso surging powerfully out of the ocean, swim the butterfly stroke? Or, if Adele was heading back to shore, how often have I stared at the hundred yards remaining to the beach—the three dogs, Heidi, Suzy, and Lily, after finding their footing on the sandy bottom and swaying slightly as if a little drunk on seawater, had come ashore and were vigorously shaking themselves —as Adele disappeared completely and breaststroked underwater. Adele could hold her breath for such a long time that, watching her, I would be certain that Adele's lungs must have burst already, at the same time that I would try to anticipate where exactly Adele's dark head would reemerge.

There! I would say to myself.

No! There!

Forty-Seven

Whoever travels without a guide
needs two hundred years for a two day journey.

—JALALUDDIN RUMI

When she had been in India barely a week, He told Adele that the time had come for her to sweep out her room. Right away, Adele borrowed a broom. She swept under the narrow iron bed, and standing on her tiptoes on the rickety wooden chair, she reached as high as she could to wipe away the cobwebs that had collected in the corners of the ceiling. Then, on her hands and knees, Adele scrubbed the floor with a stiff wire brush she had borrowed from His widowed sister-in-law. Afterwards, she went over the floor again with a dry mop. She dusted everything at least twice, her duffel bag, her books, her toiletries, and finally, balling up a sheet of newspaper, she washed the window screen until the screen squeaked.

When, at last, Adele was satisfied, she asked Gita. Gita, Adele said, would not find a single particle of dust—Gita could inspect the room wearing white gloves if she wanted to—or dirt anywhere.

After bouncing up and down a few times on Adele's narrow bed, after flipping through the pages (she stopped to read a page) of Adele's notebook which was lying on the chair, after taking down the two print rayon skirts hanging from the hook on the back of the door and holding each skirt in turn against her waist—Adele was wearing the third skirt and the T-shirt with the picture of a turtle on it that Harry had brought her back from the Okavango Delta—after inspecting the soles of the two pairs of shoes neatly lined up under the bed, after unfolding the three T-shirts folded inside the duffel bag, next to the socks and the underwear, and after rummaging inside Adele's bag of toiletries—Gita took out Adele's nonallergenic deodorant, Adele's toothpaste, Adele's face cream (she opened the jar of Oil of Olay and stuck her finger in it), Adele's toilet water (without asking permission, Gita sprayed some L'Air du Temps behind her ears, on her wrists), Gita finally said, "Adele, I am sorry but I think you must have misunderstood. What I am sure Father meant was: Sweep out your heart!"

Forty-Eight

When the ax came into the forest,
the trees said: The handle is one of us.

—A TURKISH SAYING

Another thing Adele talked about was how the women in His house—His wife, His mother-in-law, His widowed sister-in-law, Sonia, Gita even—refused to let Adele help them in the kitchen or help with the dishes. (Adele said she had tried to insist, she had told His wife, His mother-in-law, she had even argued with His widowed sister-in-law that she was used to it. Back home in Connecticut, she did all the cooking, she did all the dishes.) In addition, His wife washed all of Adele's clothes by hand, ironed them—the three print rayon skirts, the four T-shirts, her socks and underwear. Never before, Adele said, had her clothes looked cleaner, brighter. To thank her, Adele could not offer His wife money, this would have been insulting. Instead, Adele had bought His wife, His mother-in-law, His widowed sister-in-law silk sari material. And as a surprise and a luxury they would never buy for themselves, Adele had bought His two daughters, Sonia and Gita, a box of sanitary napkins.

Forty-Nine

Whenever Howard spoke of this to me or to anyone,
Howard said he refused to feel guilty—the affair with
Melissa had nothing to do with it. On the contrary,
Howard felt that he was being more than generous.
But the real problem, he said, had nothing to do with
the money—paying for Adele's accommodations at the
Caribbean resort, paying for her airplane ticket from
India, paying (and arranging) for the three Irish setters

to fly to her there—but with how Adele had changed. One of Howard's constant refrains. Howard said he could remember the days when Adele liked nothing better than to ride her horse, Sylvia Plath, the days when Adele would drop everything to play three sets of tennis with him, or still more clearly, Howard could remember the days when nothing could have kept Adele from swimming every day—hadn't Howard built and heated the pool in Connecticut especially for her?

And Adele took care of herself then. Adele dressed well. Adele did not go around wearing old T-shirts and faded shapeless skirts. Adele used to be a good-looking woman. In the street, Howard said, people—and not just men—would turn around to look at her, to stare at Adele. Adele had style, Adele had what-did-you-call-it? presence.

What was more, Howard said, Adele, believe it or not, liked to go out—out to dinner, out to restaurants. Adele, often, was the very last person to leave the dance floor. Sometimes, if Adele was having a good time, if Adele had drunk a couple of glasses of wine, Howard said, he literally had to drag Adele home, and Howard said how he was thinking also of the time after Adele had run the marathon.

But according to what Adele told me while we were sitting there on the beach, Howard, her husband, could afford to be generous. Not only did Howard make a lot of money on his investments, Howard had inherited a lot more. Howard's father had made millions, maybe billions, in the real estate business in Illinois, and when Howard's father died, he left most of his money to Howard, to Howard's sister, and to the Chicago Symphony. Howard's father had also set up trust funds for his five grandchildren (Howard's sister had three children), which meant that Harry and Nina had more than enough money to live on. Harry and Nina, Adele claimed, were a lot richer than she was.

Fifty

"Aren't you hungry?" I said. Adele and I were having lunch in the restaurant high up on the cliff. "The swimming, the sun, the sea air, have given me a huge appetite."

To the waiter I said, "I'm going to have the tomato and basil soup to start with, then the cold lobster salad. Oh, yes, and a glass of white wine."

When the food arrived, Adele only picked at

hers—Adele had ordered a vegetable salad—and she took tiny sips from her glass of mineral water as if the water was hard for her to swallow.

"You must miss the food. The food in India. The spices, the curries. The fruit—mangoes, papayas, litchi nuts. You should try the mango ice cream. The mango ice cream, here, is delicious," I told Adele. "This wine, too," I said, taking a sip.

Looking past me at the Caribbean, Adele said, "I haven't had a drink since I met Him. I haven't eaten any meat, poultry, or fish either. The only thing I miss from time to time is a cigarette—and the strange thing is that I never used to smoke much anyway. My father smoked. My father smoked a pack a day, and the other strange thing," Adele continued, "is that He knew right away without my having to tell Him that my father died of drink and that I was the one who found him lying on the living room floor holding an empty bottle of gin. I tried to give my father mouth-to-mouth resuscitation, but it was too late already. His lungs had filled with fluid. When the paramedics arrived, one of them said to me that the same thing happened if someone drowned."

Fifty-One

O brother, you are your very thought
As for the rest, you are only hair and bone.
If your thought is a rose, you're a garden of roses.
If it's a thorn, you're but fuel for the stove.

—JALALUDDIN RUMI

In Bombay, there was a large department store He
always made a point of going to. In fact, if He had His
way, He liked to joke, He would spend His entire day
there. He said He liked to ride the escalator up to
every floor and He liked to inspect the new
merchandise, the kitchen utensils especially, which
were well displayed—the Cuisinarts, the coffee
grinders, the gadgets to purée vegetables, to core

apples, and to slice hard-boiled eggs. In addition, the time Adele had gone with Him, He said all the sales-people were so helpful.

First, He bought a Corning Ware casserole dish for His wife, then He spent nearly an hour choosing an Egyptian-cotton dress shirt for Ramji. Should the shirt be white or have stripes? He asked for Adele's advice. And should the collar be narrow and pointed, or more fashionably, be smaller, wider? Should the shirt have French cuffs or simply a button? Already, dozens of men's shirts lay unfolded and on top of each other on the counter while, with the salesman—by then several salesmen had gathered around to give their opinions— He discussed the merits of each shirt as if He were choosing a rare and priceless antique.

Impatient, Adele had wandered away. Across the hall, in the ladies' department, she noticed a pleated skirt which, according to the label, one could wash, then just twist and let dry, and the pleats would always come out perfectly. Adele was tempted, and the skirt was not expensive—at home, in Connecticut, she would not have hesitated. But here, in India, Adele did not want to appear greedy, acquisitive. And after all, she told herself, three skirts were probably plenty.

When, after only a few minutes—quickly, she

had gone and tried on the pleated skirt—Adele went back to the men's shirt counter to rejoin Him, He was no longer there. She looked for Him everywhere— down all the aisles, in each department, on every floor —but could not find Him. When Adele asked the salesman—a Sikh in a turban, the same salesman, she was certain—if he had seen Him, the Sikh salesman shook his head. The Sikh salesman, when Adele questioned him further, seemed to have no recollection of Him or of the mound of shirts that Adele swore, just a few moments ago, had littered the counter in front of them both. *Sorry, madam,* the salesman kept repeating and shaking his turbaned head.

Adele began to argue. She began to shout. Several other salesmen appeared and, likewise, each volubly denied having seen Him or having helped Him buy a shirt or, for that matter, any item. Eventually, the store manager was called for, and very politely, very quietly, he made it clear to Adele that she had to leave the department store.

Firmly taking Adele by the elbow, while everyone in the department store stopped what they were doing, stopped what they were buying to take a good look at her, the store manager ushered Adele down the escalator and out the front door.

Afterwards, when Adele had caught up with Him (holding a bulging shopping bag, He was waiting for her on the street corner), and barely able to restrain her tears, she complained to Him that never in her whole life had she felt so ashamed, so humiliated, and that everyone in that department store must have thought she was a shoplifter, He reached down and, from the bulging shopping bag, He extracted the pleated skirt.

"Now, you must return it!" He said to Adele.

Fifty-Two

Had he already told me, Howard asked me on the same day I went to his office and saw the framed photograph he still keeps on his desk of Adele, about the last time he and Adele went out to a restaurant? An expensive restaurant, a restaurant at which Howard had had to make a reservation days in advance, and had he already told me about Adele's new black dress? The black dress had this low-cut back and the black dress, as far as Howard knew, was still hanging in her closet in Connecticut unless the moths had gotten to it. In any case, what Howard was trying to tell me was how Adele looked.

Adele looked beautiful, Howard said.

And everyone was having a good time—they had had a few drinks at the bar, their friends had arrived on time, the table was in the right corner of the room, they had ordered their food—and Howard would never forget, he said, how he said to himself, to hell with my diet for this one night, and he had ordered roast goat, the restaurant's specialty, and ravioli with truffles to start with, when, all of a sudden, Adele in this melodramatic way had thrown back her head—I should have seen her, Howard said—her elbows pointing high up in the air, so that the two men sitting next to her had to lean away, and she had started by taking off the cultured pearl necklace that she had put on to go with the black dress. Next, Adele took off the emerald and diamond earrings in the shape of a shell that Howard had given her for their fifteenth wedding anniversary—this had taken a little longer, Adele had pierced ears—and she set the earrings down next to the pearl necklace on the table. Then, as everyone watched—the whole table, all their friends, had fallen silent (maybe, as far as Howard knew, everyone in the whole restaurant was watching too)—Adele pulled from her finger the valuable pear-shaped diamond engagement ring that had belonged to Howard's mother.

"Adele!" Too late, Howard had tried to warn her.

Reaching for her fork to begin her salad, Adele had accidentally knocked one of the emerald-and-diamond earrings in the shape of a shell to the floor just as the waiter came up to their table to pour the wine into their glasses. And the crack under his heel, Howard said, could not have been any more distinct or any more final than if a bullet had been fired at close range.

"And it cost me five thousand dollars," Howard said.

Fifty-Three

When Harry went all the way out to India to visit Adele, he lost his luggage. Or, more precisely, the airline lost it. For some unclear reason (since it was tagged properly), Harry's brown canvas suitcase was taken off the plane in Bangkok where, unclaimed, it probably went round and round on the carousel until it was the only piece of luggage left. Eventually, the carousel stopped and eventually, too, a porter must have taken the suitcase off the carousel and taken it over to the unclaimed luggage office. There, the official, his feet propped up on his desk, was busy cleaning his ear with his pinky fingernail—grown and left long precisely for this purpose—and he nodded to the porter to set the suitcase down. After he had finished cleaning his other ear and without giving Harry's brown suitcase a glance, the official left the office—carefully locking the door behind him—to buy himself a bowl of noodles for lunch and to play a quick hand of poker with the air traffic controllers.

In Bombay, Harry's final destination, Harry berated not only the airline official whom he was speaking to—no, yelling at—but also the airline, the whole country of India, the entire Third World. Harry had traveled a great deal—to Europe, to Africa, to the Caribbean—and nothing like this, he said, had ever happened to him.

To Adele, when, after taking the crowded train from Bombay, he finally arrived in the taxi—in the heat, the dust, the maze of unmarked streets, unnumbered houses—Harry complained that he did not even have a toothbrush with him. After the long flight, what he would not give for a shave, a cold shower, a clean shirt, he said.

Adele laughed. Adele told Harry how it did not matter. Adele said Harry must have lost his suitcase for a good reason. Harry, she said, was probably too attached to the suitcase and to what was in it. Adele said how, in a way, wasn't it ironic that this should happen to Harry here in India? Harry did not know how to answer Adele.

Oh, Ma, don't. Just look at the skirt you're wearing, he said to her.

The trip he felt was doomed from the start and he should never have come. What had he thought? Had he thought he could talk Adele into coming back home with him? Had he thought he could talk Adele into resuming her old life—cooking, shopping for clothes, thinking about art?

Yet, after only three days, Adele was right. Harry could no longer recall what was inside his brown canvas suitcase. Harry borrowed a clean shirt from Ramji, and Ramji, it also turned out, had nearly the same size feet and he lent Harry a pair of comfortable brown sandals. Harry had gone out and bought himself a new toothbrush, a new razor (he liked the new razor better), he had gotten used to the vegetarian food, he looked forward to eating the *chapatis,* the couscous, and to eating with only the tips of the fingers of his right hand. He hardly noticed the absence of alcohol, the heat was not as bad as he had anticipated—at that time of year, it was cool enough to need a blanket in bed at night—and he got along especially well with Sonia, the married daughter. Sonia, Harry told Adele, had a wonderful sense of humor. Each time Sonia had to ask her father something, she prefaced her question with: *Father, if you are in your body now—* In actuality, Harry could not think of anything else he needed in India.

Only when Harry had been back in the States for several weeks and he had almost forgotten about his lost suitcase did he get a call from the airline saying that they had finally been able to locate it for him.

When the suitcase arrived, Harry told the airline deliveryman that another mistake had been made. The suitcase was not his. His suitcase was brown, canvas, relatively new. This suitcase was black, old, missing a handle. Inside the suitcase, too, the contents did not look like anything Harry would own: children's clothes, a pink plastic doll, a package of Chinese condoms.

Fifty-Four

One of the first things Nina said she asked Harry,
when he got back from India, was about Adele's
hair—"Is Mom's hair still curly and short?" was
what Nina said she asked—but Harry said he did
not know, he said he had not paid particular
attention. Harry told Nina that if he remembered
correctly, Adele's hair was a lot shorter, and

Adele's hair had a bit of white in it—no, Harry had called it silver—but that he, Harry, could not swear to it.

Instead, Harry told Nina what he would never forget was how one morning he had watched Him sit outside in the garden with a towel draped over His shoulders while Adele had cut His hair. Adele, Harry said—and Nina might have a hard time believing this—had gotten good at it. (The first time she cut His hair, Adele had confessed to Harry, her hand shook so hard she was afraid she would cut off His ear.) Adele had a pair of haircutting scissors that she got specially sharpened, and that she did not use for anything else. (One time, she found His grandson using the scissors to cut out a picture of Madonna from *Time* magazine, and Adele had wanted to slap him—nothing dulls scissors faster than paper!)

Also, Adele admitted to keeping the hair clippings. The hair clippings, Harry told Nina, reminded him of when he and Nina were little and Adele was still living in Connecticut and Howard would trim the hair on the three Irish setters with a pair of electric clippers. (After Adele had left for India, Harry said he found a burlap bag filled with the Irish setters' red hair in the basement.)

The other thing that happened to Harry in India was when Harry asked his mother, Adele, if she would now cut *his* hair, Adele shook her head.

Fifty-Five

Although it was hard for her to like Francis Bacon—
like his paintings was what she said she meant—Nina
said to me the day I went to talk to her about the dog,
Lily, in her studio downtown, Francis Bacon was a
great painter. And in the book she was reading about
him, which was a collection of interviews, Francis
Bacon had said that, basically, art is an accident,
and in trying to do a portrait, for instance, Francis

Bacon told the interviewer, ideally he wished that he could just pick up a handful of paint and throw it at the canvas and hope the portrait would be there. Francis Bacon actually did throw paint at his canvas, and for texture, he threw dirt and dust from his studio on the canvas as well—there was a photograph of Francis Bacon's studio in the book, and sure enough, Nina said, Francis Bacon's studio looked filthy! Nina told me how she had tried to do the same thing, throw paint on the canvas, but the result, she said, was a big mess.

"But what has this got to do with your mother, Adele?" I wanted to know then.

Fifty-Six

Adele never did answer Howard when Howard kept asking Adele what else she did in Bangkok for those ten days besides getting her hair cut.

Likewise, *Only the radio!* Adele had finally answered her mother, who had shouted at her through the locked door the first time Adele brought her boyfriend, Paul, home from school with her. Adele was fifteen at the time, and Adele had taken a bottle of gin out of her father's liquor cabinet—later she would water down the gin so that her father would not notice how much was missing—and she and Paul had shut themselves up in Adele's bedroom. Lying side by side on Adele's bed, they took turns taking swigs of gin straight from the bottle and Paul had held Adele so tightly in his arms that he came in his pants against her.

Ssh, Adele kept telling Paul.

Ssh.

At other times, Adele and Paul did, in fact, listen to the radio. To the replay of *I Can Hear it Now,* and Adele especially liked the sound of the reporter's voice breaking—"It's tragic, terrible . . . Oh, my, get out of the way, please . . . Four, five hundred feet into the sky . . . It's a terrific crash, ladies and gentlemen . . . the smoke and the flames, now . . . all the humanity"—when the *Hindenburg* burst into flames. Or else they would listen to a recording of wolf calls which Adele and Paul would then try to imitate.

"Although the wolf has acquired the reputation of being an aggressive predator that we associate with . . ." a voice would drone on while Paul was rolling a joint and while Adele was buttoning up her blouse. (Adele said she and Paul spent hours necking in the basement of Paul's parents' house.) Often, as

Paul was lighting up the marijuana joint—Adele swore she did cocaine only twice in her life—upstairs the phone would start to ring. "Don't answer it," Adele would whisper to him.

"Hoo hoo hoo." Baring his teeth and snarling, Paul would go first.

Adele's turn next; she inhaled deeply, coughed slightly. "Hoo hoo hoo hoo."

"Hoo hoo hoo hoo." Paul exhaled a stream of marijuana smoke. Cautiously sniffing the air, he cocked his head appearing to be listening intently to something. Then, turning toward Adele, he made a slow batting motion with his hand as if he were teasing or playing, before suddenly jumping up, his arms and legs spread-eagled in the air.

"Hoo hoo hoo no no!" Adele shrieked in mock and real terror as, still holding the joint in her hand, she drew her knees up against her chest.

Letting himself drop heavily on top of Adele, Paul noisily started to lick Adele's face and ears with his tongue.

"Hoo hoo ha ha ha!" Adele could not stop laughing as, upstairs, the telephone started to ring again. This time, it rang for a long time.

Fifty-Seven

Question: What is the realization which is beyond
understanding?
Maharaj: Imagine a deep jungle full of tigers and you in
a strong steel cage. Knowing that you are well protected by
the cage, you watch the tigers fearlessly.
Next you find the tigers in the cage and yourself roaming
the jungle. Last—the cage disappears and you
ride the tigers!

— SRI NISARGADATTA MAHARAJ

In Bangkok, Adele had nothing to do while she waited
to catch the next plane. Every two or three hours she
would go and telephone Air India, but each time, a
recorded message in several different languages told
her what she knew already: the airport was shut, the
airlines were on strike still. Then, out of boredom and
frustration probably, Adele went to find a restaurant, a
coffee shop, or she would stop off at a street vendor

(the more she ate, the hungrier she got) to buy fried bananas, pancakes, a bowl of noodles, a plate of glutinous rice topped with coconut milk and sliced mangoes (it was the season for them).

Everywhere she went during those ten days (to Adele, those ten days seemed like ten years!)—walking around Wat Po, climbing to the top of Wat Arun, crossing the Chao Phya River in a tippy wooden boat, standing in front of the Emerald Buddha, looking up at the kite-flying in Lumpini Park, watching roosters fight on Sunday at the Pramane Grounds—Adele was always chewing on something or getting ready to put a spoon or wield a pair of chopsticks up to her mouth.

Adele ate peppers so hot she stopped breathing, betel nuts that stained her lips dark crimson, thousand-year-old duck eggs soaked in horses' urine, rooster testicles, the meat of the nearly extinct barking deer, bulls'-balls soup, durian-flavored ice cream, in other words, Adele, her stomach always bloated, always distended—how many pounds had she gained already? five? ten?—tried eating everything.

Each day the waistbands of her printed rayon skirts were tighter and tighter, harder and harder to button. The cotton T-shirts were stretched over her expanding belly, over her all-of-a-sudden-burgeoning breasts. For the first time in her life, Adele was getting plump. Adele was getting fat.

In the street, men turned to look her up and down once, twice, three times. They shouted out things to her that Adele could not understand, although she, of course, could guess what they meant. One time, a man on a bicycle riding past her as she was walking along Sukhumvit Road had reached over and tried to grab Adele's ass. Another man had followed her all the way down New Road to the post office so that, exasperated, Adele had turned around and yelled: "Leave me alone, goddammit!"

Adele had yelled so loudly that a man who was walking down New Road had stopped. "Adele? Is that you, Adele? Adele, what a coincidence! Adele, I nearly didn't recognize you!" he said.

Adele, too, nearly did not recognize Jim Baronio. Jim Baronio was her neighbor in Connecticut (once, Jim Baronio had complained to Howard about the three dogs running over his lawn). Jim Baronio told Adele that he was in Bangkok on business, he told Adele that he was glad to see her and how well she looked—had she gained a pound or two? If so, it suited her—and he invited Adele out to dinner.

They went to an expensive Western-style restaurant (Jim Baronio said that he knew better than to eat Thai food, he knew better than to eat any Oriental food), where they drank two bottles of French wine and where Adele ordered duck liver pâté to start with, rock lobster in a heavy cream sauce for an entrée, and chocolate mousse cake for dessert. Afterwards, Jim Baronio took Adele to a nightclub on Patpong Road that he said someone had recommended to him and the last thing Adele remembered from that evening was drinking her gin and tonic and watching the floor show (a woman was blowing perfect smoke rings out of her vagina) while Jim Baronio was stroking her hair and telling her how soft it felt.

In the morning when Adele woke up, she had a terrible headache. Also, she was in Jim Baronio's hotel room, she was in Jim Baronio's bed. Jim Baronio was lying next to her, and as quickly and as quietly as she could—Adele's heart was pounding so loudly she was afraid it would wake him up (once, Jim Baronio had stretched out his arm and said something that sounded like *Okay, okay, give me your money!* and turned over)— Adele had gotten up, gotten dressed.

Adele just made it back to her hotel room in the nick of time before she had diarrhea and had to throw up both at the same time. (Without a moment to lose,

Adele had to make up her mind whether to sit on the toilet or hang her head over it.)

The next day, Adele felt so weak she could hardly lift her head off the pillow, let alone get out of bed. She was retching emptily and painfully into a spittoon she had dragged into her room from the hotel hallway. The spittoon was full of tobacco juice and cigarette butts, but by then Adele was too sick to care. Nor did she care that her sheets were stained and that her room stank. Except for drinking some bottled water (the first time, Adele drank it too fast and threw up again), she did not eat anything all day. Still worse, she was to say later, was that in spite of herself, Adele kept thinking about food—about deviled eggs. Dozens of deviled eggs set out on a platter—the bright yellow yolks formed into peaks and sprinkled with cayenne. The thought of them made her stomach cramp, her throat gag.

The yellow also made Adele think of the time the three dogs, Heidi, Suzy, and Lily, had eaten the remains of an animal they had dug up somewhere in the garden, and afterwards, to make themselves throw up, the dogs had eaten grass. The grass, when it came up, was wrapped in a bright yellow film of slime that, to this day and no matter how many times or how hard

Adele had tried to clean it, had left an ugly stain on the off-white carpet in the living room of the house.

Adele could not remember how long exactly she stayed in bed—one, two, three days? The shades were drawn and day and night melded together. Above her bed, the fan whirred ceaselessly. A maid knocked from time to time; Adele sent her away. It was always too hot and Adele was too tired. Too tired to get out of bed, except to go to the bathroom.

Mainly, Adele slept.

On the second or perhaps it was the third day, finally, Adele ran herself a bath. Standing naked in front of the full-length mirror in the bathroom, she examined herself carefully. She was relieved to see that her stomach was concave, her hipbones stuck out, she was flat-chested again. Later, when she got dressed, her clothes fit her loosely, they buttoned easily the way they used to—the T-shirt she had worn when she ran the marathon in under four hours, the flower-print skirt. Only, her hair hung in too long, thin wisps, the curl gone out of it. When she tried to brush it back, it fell into her eyes; when she tried to tie it up in a ponytail, it was not long enough.

Outside in the hot, crowded street, it took Adele a few moments to realize that all the stores, all the restaurants—by now, she was hungry, she was looking for a place where she could drink some tea, eat a bowl of plain rice—were shut. In the street, too, people looked different to her, they were acting strangely, shouting, laughing, waving their arms, dancing almost, and again, it took Adele a while to figure out why— most of the people in the street were wet, their clothes, their shoes, their hair, all sopping wet.

Adele kept walking, she felt light-headed—the heat, the sun, the lack of food. Once or twice, some-one started to throw water on her and at the last minute stopped—*farang!* She was a foreigner, it would not count, it would not bring her good luck.

Eventually, she found herself walking down a wide avenue which she recognized as being the route to the airport. Stalls had been set up which sold souve-nirs, jasmine leis, sticky pink sweets, small brown birds inside bamboo cages to be released as instant good deeds. On the sidewalk, a man sitting at a porta-ble desk was writing letters for a fee, a barber was giving a young priest a haircut. As Adele walked by them, out of the corner of her eye, she caught sight of an Air India bus driving past.

When the barber had finished—the young priest had paid, left—Adele went and sat herself down in the barber's chair, an ordinary wooden chair. She gestured that she, too, wanted her hair cut, all of it, any which way, any old way would do, she told the barber in English, it did not matter to her, she would pay double —the barber was looking at her curiously—and to show him, with one hand she grabbed a handful of her hair, then another handful, while with her other hand she made wild snipping motions in the air—CUT, CUT, CUT.

Fifty-Eight

I should have told Adele then—Adele and I were
walking on the beach, the three Irish setters, Heidi,
Suzy, and Lily, running along with us—that when I
was young I, too, was obsessed, I wanted to be a ballet
dancer more than I wanted to be anything else. I
should have told Adele that I, too, had covered all the
walls of my bedroom with pasted-up pictures, only the

pictures were of Maria Tallchief, Margot Fonteyn, Tanaquil Leclerq doing *tour jetés, fouettés, arabesques,* and I should have said then how when I went to bed at night, to achieve my own turnout, I tied my feet to the posts at the foot of my bed.

Instead, I talked about how, for the first time, I had noticed that there were clouds in the sky. Large, slow-moving, white cumulus clouds, and that as a result, the sea did not look the same blue, but was dappled with patches of yellow, patches of gray. The water, too, I commented to Adele, seemed denser, as if overnight it had amassed more weight, more volume. When I had gone in for a quick dip and peered down at the usually clear sandy bottom, the bottom seemed murky, I said. And when, earlier, I had remarked on this same thing to the French boy, the French boy said that this was a sign of a change in the weather. The change usually coincided with the phases of the moon, and the moon, he said, would be full soon.

Of course, Adele had gone swimming that day, the way she always did, with Heidi, Suzy, and Lily swimming along with her. And although I don't remember my exact words to her and whether I shouted them out to her from where I was standing on the beach, in any case my words made no difference (or perhaps my words were carried away by the wind and Adele did not hear them), because it seemed to me as if Adele was gone much longer that day, as if Adele and her three dogs swam out much further that day.

Fifty-Nine

While Adele was in India, Nina wrote several letters to her mother. This letter was dated back in July.

Dearest Mom,

Yesterday, Dad and Melissa took me to lunch at a French restaurant for my birthday which meant that I had to put on a dress! I wore my red sandals (too hot for stockings!) with the straps that crisscross at the ankle that we bought together the time you bought the see-through shoes, remember? and Dad said I looked really nice, for a change! I ordered the shrimp to begin with—the waiter said the shrimp came from Puget Sound (Puget Sound and Vancouver Island are where I want to go next summer— you could meet me there! Okay?) For the main course, I had the cold pasta with green and yellow and red peppers —good, but not as good as the shrimp. Dad had the consommé and cold tongue—the trouble with tongue is that it really looks like a tongue. As usual, he says he is on a diet. Dad's hair has gotten much grayer since the last time. He definitely looks older. You know how people kind of look the same for years and years until all of a sudden, whammo! in a single day, they look twenty years older. Melissa was wearing a yellow linen suit that did not have a single wrinkle in it—the story of her face. We talked about Harry's getting a job and my not having a job (!)—Dad refuses to recognize the ARTS as a possible source of income. Ha! He is right. When Melissa went to "powder her nose" (she actually said this) Dad leaned over and said to me in his most intimate charming (read: do-not-contradict-me) CEO voice: "So, tell me, how is your mother doing these days?"

    I said: "Fine. Mom is just fine, Dad. Mom is in a

small village in India somewhere, Mom is living with a guru in an ashram with no indoor plumbing and she is sleeping on the floor on a grass mat with malaria mosquitoes buzzing and zooming around her head, she is eating nothing but rice with her fingers and because she has given away everything she owns including her shoes, she is walking barefoot in the mud paddies and the half-starving nothing-but-skin-and-bones cows standing in the middle of the road have more to eat than Mom does. Why do you ask, Dad?''

No. I didn't say this. Just kidding!

Mom? Are you there?

When are you coming home? Mom?

I guess you know by now that Harry is moving out to San Francisco. He says he is already planning his skiing vacations to Aspen, Tahoe, Snowbird, and India. How's the snow out there?

Right now, it is hotter than hell in the city. I finally broke down and bought myself an air conditioner: I sleep, eat, paint in the bedroom—what is so great about northern light anyway? Mark and I have decided not to see each other so much anymore—whatever that means! The meaning, I guess, will reveal itself—isn't that what you always say?

In the book that you gave me, I read a story about

an old man who on his deathbed tells his sons that gold is buried in the fields—did you read that story, Mom? The sons go out and dig and dig and find nothing, so instead they plant wheat and they get rich anyhow. Great!

Everything in the art world has shut down for the summer, but I ran into someone who has a share in a new gallery that is going to open down here and he said for me to bring my work around in the fall so, maybe—keep your fingers crossed for me . . . Also, the guy with the gallery has these nice blue eyes.

I am supposed to be at the Seurat exhibit in half an hour so I better get going. Seurat is not my favorite artist. (Who is? Hard question. At the moment, a toss-up between Leonardo da Vinci and Richard Diebenkorn!) At least, it will be nice and cool in the museum . . .

I love you.

Nina

P.S. One more story: A man swims the Tigris River every night to be with his beloved. One night, for the first time, he notices a mole on the beloved's face. That night, the beloved warns him not to cross the river for he will drown.

Do you know that story? I like the first one better.

Write to me!

Don't forget we have a date to meet in Puget Sound next summer!

Adele never received the letter—perhaps Nina never sent it.

Sixty

When Adele decided that she was going to leave once and for all, she packed her small suitcase and drove off without saying a word to Howard or to anyone (Nina and Harry were away already). She did not even stop on her way out the door to pat the three dogs (this would have been too painful for her), who were sleeping on their beds under the kitchen table. It was raining, Adele said, and it was in the middle of the night, and Adele, of course, drove much too fast.

The highway patrolman who pulled her over (Adele was so intent on her own thoughts that she did not notice the lights flashing behind her car, the patrolman had had to drive alongside and yell at her through his megaphone) maintained that she was driving at eighty-two miles an hour.

"What's your big hurry, lady?" the patrolman had asked.

Adele had started to cry then. In between painful hiccups and the frequent blowing of her nose, she told the patrolman that the reason she was driving over the speed limit was that, after nearly twenty years of marriage, she was leaving her husband.

The patrolman, a young man—much younger than Adele, certainly—in his late twenties or early thirties, had said to Adele, "Okay, okay, lady. Please, stop crying and, this one time, I'll let you off. I won't give you a speeding ticket if, first, you follow me."

In his car—the blue lights on the roof still flashing importantly—the young patrolman led Adele to an all-night diner off the highway. There, he bought Adele breakfast: pancakes, syrup, fried eggs, coffee, bacon, juice, everything.

When Adele was finishing her second cup of coffee and was soaking up the last forkful of pancake in the last bit of syrup—she had stopped crying and was smiling—the young patrolman said: "That's more like it, Adele. To me, now, you look like someone who is ready to make a rational decision and drive back home to her husband at fifty-five miles an hour."

Adele had thanked the young patrolman. "You are right," she told him, "the big breakfast was just what I needed to make a rational decision."

But as soon as Adele was back in her car, as soon as Adele had smiled and waved goodbye, and as soon as the young patrolman had left, the blue lights on the roof of his car flashing importantly once more, Adele had continued to drive in the same exact direction and at the same exact speed—at eighty-two miles an hour.

Sixty-One

Without your speech the soul has no ear,
without your ear the soul has no tongue.

—JALALUDDIN RUMI

The whole time Adele was in India, she never got to
see it once, she said—oh, yes, she nearly forgot,
except for that one time from twenty thousand feet!
The pilot, on a flight from Bombay to Delhi, had
announced that the passengers seated on the
right-hand side of the aircraft, if they looked down,
could see it. Adele said this kind of thing always
happened to her: Hoover Dam, the Grand Canyon,

Mont Blanc, the game inside Shea Stadium—she had seen them all out of plane windows.

Rarely would He sightsee. He said that there was more than plenty to see inside His own heart, more than enough to fill the whole of the Metropolitan Museum, the Victoria and Albert, the Prado, and the Louvre combined.

Instead, Adele said, she had bought a picture postcard of it. For a while, and before He said not to, she had Scotch-taped the postcard to the wall of her small bedroom. The postcard was one of those old-fashioned pastel-colored, touched-up photographs in which two women holding open parasols were standing next to the reflecting pool. On the crenelated white border, in fine gold slanted script, was written, *Agra, India, 1919.*

Adele had looked at this picture so often and so much that she could let herself into it:

The heat. My dear, have you ever felt such heat? first, the light blue woman on the right would sigh.

The heat. And the filth. The filth and the flies, the pale green woman on the left would murmur back, at the same time that she would give her parasol an impatient little twirl.

After Adele had given the two women names,

ages, husbands, children, miscarriages, she decided
that she had gone as far as she could go with them. She
took down the Taj Mahal, and before filling the avail-
able space with *BLUE BLUE BLUE BLUE* in large block
letters and mailing it to Jim Baronio in Connecticut—
her neighbor, how could she ever forget the address!
—Adele used the stiff edges of the postcard to clean
out her fingernails.

Sixty-Two

Howard, too, it turned out, got a picture postcard
—a postcard of van Gogh's sunflowers. The postcard
was mailed from somewhere in India; Howard could
not read the postmark, he said. The message on the
postcard was a drawn-in square where all the
numbers add up to 15.

4	9	2
3	5	7
8	1	6

At the bottom of the square, Adele had marked two crosses and signed a capital *A* for her name.

After he had studied the postcard for a while, Howard put the postcard faceup on the kitchen floor next to the three dogs' bowls for Heidi, Suzy, and Lily to sniff at.

Sixty-Three

Question: When an ordinary man dies, what happens to
him?
Maharaj: According to his belief it happens. As life
before that is but imagination, so is life after. The dream
continues.

—SRI NISARGADATTA MAHARAJ

Perhaps it was not entirely accidental that soon after
Harry left (some days, in India, Adele missed her son,
Harry, more than she missed anyone), Adele began to
suffer from irregular heartbeats, an uncomfortable
sensation she compared to having a fluttering bird
trapped inside her chest. Adele would turn pale then,
she would suddenly have to catch her breath.

At night, when Adele lay down in her bed, the bird—a small bird, a nondescript brownish-gray bird that she thought might be a sparrow—intensified his fluttering. In addition, Adele heard a buzzing sound and she had a strange tingling sensation in her toes, in her fingertips. She convinced herself that these were the sure signs of an impending heart attack.

Should she warn someone? Adele had wondered. Should she confide her fears to Him, or would He mock and accuse her of being a silly hypochondriac? Of being another spoiled foreigner? Instead, Adele made a mental note of her possessions and to whom she would leave them: Sonia and Gita, His daughters, could share her toiletries (including the deodorant and the bottle of L'Air du Temps); Ramji could have her books and papers; her clothes—the sweater she had traveled in, which for the moment, she had misplaced (Adele was afraid she had left it in a taxi in Bombay), the three skirts, her four T-shirts, her sandals that needed to be resoled and her brown walking shoes, her socks and her underwear—should be distributed amongst the poor. In her head, Adele wrote a brief but poignant farewell letter to her children, Harry and Nina.

Adele did not want to die quite yet, but she tried to be fatalistic. Better to die simply here in India, she told herself, where death was not such a big affair. Better to die here naturally than to go back to America and submit herself to a battery of painful, expensive, and unnecessary procedures and tests. In India, people were used to death, people faced death every day and everywhere—even small children were not impressed by death. Death was routine. Death was real while life was the illusion—*samsara*.

Adele had only to look around her at the people in the market, in the street: beggars with their running sores and missing limbs, old women with their brittle bones and fallen bellies, undernourished children clamoring around her and trying to draw her attention with their too large, dark eyes and their dry feverish fingers. By comparison, how could she be so afraid of a little bird inside her chest? Adele scolded herself into making the best of the days still left to her.

But curiously, once Adele was asleep, Adele slept well. She had never slept better. She slept soundly, dreamlessly. She slept right through the warm humid nights, seven hours, sometimes more, eight, nine hours. She barely moved—the sheets on her bed showed no crease.

In the morning, however, first thing when she woke up and before the bird trapped inside her chest began to beat its frantic wings and frighten her again, Adele would pinch the flesh on her arm hard and ask herself: "Hey! Are you alive still?"

Sixty-Four

A hundred torrents rise
From the surge my soul within;
The heavens in glad surprise
Stand still to behold me spin.

— RUBAIYAT

In India, on a day Adele thought might be Christmas
Eve—Adele no longer kept track of time, of what
day of the week, of what month of the year it was
—He had put a tape into the machine. He had
turned up the volume.

Adele had to go stand in the middle of the room.
The way she was standing, she could have been a ballet

dancer, she could have been one of Martha Graham's modern dancers. Her back was rigid, her shoulders were thrown back, her arms were crossed over her flat chest, each hand clasped the opposite bony shoulder.

Slowly, Adele had started to turn. She had turned clockwise. Her right foot was pointed, her leg extended. Bent slightly at the neck, her head did not budge.

Her full skirt billowed out, and at each turn, the wooden floor creaked under her bare feet.

Adele turned past the rattan armchair with its faded yellow linen pillows on which He was sitting, Adele turned past the glass coffee table piled high with old magazines, Adele turned past the other rattan armchair on which Ramji was sitting with his little son perched on his knee, Adele turned past the door to the kitchen where, standing together and giggling, Sonia and Gita had parted the wood-bead curtain to look at her.

The next time around, Adele went faster so that His face, the faces of Ramji, his little son, Sonia, and Gita were blurred. Then again, faster, faster she turned.

"Feliz Navidad, feliz Navidad," Adele kept singing softly to herself, while He and Ramji clapped their hands in time to the loud music.

He clapped and clapped and would not let Adele stop. He made Adele turn and turn until she dropped.

Sixty-Five

The sky was a solid mass of gray clouds and it was raining hard. The rain was leaking through the thatched bungalow roofs and dripping onto the blue-and-green-cotton sofa cushions, the rain was seeping through the striped awning over the restaurant high up on the cliff, soaking the linen tablecloths and folded napkins and making the tile floor slippery and shiny. (The little yellow sugar birds that hopped from table to table were nowhere in sight.) All the orange, red, and purple flowers on the hibiscus, the oleander, and the bougainvillea bushes had been blown off by gusts of rain and lay on the ground, shriveled and scentless.

Adele was the only person on the beach—even the French boy had not come around that day on account of the rain—and from where I was sitting on the patio of my bungalow, I watched her and the three dogs, Heidi, Suzy, and Lily, go in swimming.

Like the sky that day, the ocean was dark gray, the dark green-gray of beaten metal, with high-peaked waves surging and breaking unpredictably everywhere, and I could not help but say out loud to myself: "This time for sure one of those poor dogs is going to drown —the smallest one. Suzy, probably." But after a while, since I could no longer see Adele and her three dogs or follow their progress in the ocean—it was damp outside on the patio and the driving rain, too, made for poor visibility—I got up from where I was sitting and went inside my bungalow to the little kitchenette to fix myself a drink.

It was still raining, raining harder even—I had had another drink by then—when Adele, in her red two-piece bathing suit, finally emerged from the high, dashing waves and stepped onto the beach. The three

Irish setters shook themselves vigorously and I saw Adele—she may not have been tired or out of breath, she may have been smiling, too far away, I could not tell—automatically, with one hand, brush the short hair from her face, at the same time that I swear I heard her say—her voice carried by the wind all the way to where I was sitting holding my drink, "Short hair is better for swimming anyway."

Sixty-Six

Not only the thirsty seek the water,
the water as well seeks the thirsty.

—JALALUDDIN RUMI

The list of Adele's sins did not satisfy Him. The list, He told Adele, was incomplete. A sin was missing from it.

The sin, Adele believed, was not hers but Ramji's.

Sixty-Seven

Once Chuang-tzu dreamt that he was a butterfly,
fluttering around, happy with himself and absolutely
carefree. He didn't know he was Chuang-tzu. Suddenly,
he woke up: there he was in the flesh; unmistakably
Chuang-tzu. But he didn't know if he was Chuang-tzu
who had just dreamt that he was a butterfly or a
butterfly now dreaming that he was Chuang-tzu.

— CHUANG-TZU

One night when the dogs in the street would not
stop barking and it was too hot to sleep, Adele
heard her door open. Someone came in.

"Who is—" she started to say.

"Ssh." Ramji had let himself in.

"What is—" Adele tried to say again. In
bed, she sat up. Ramji put his hand over her
mouth.

213

. . .

In the morning, Gita was pouring her her tea and Sonia, Ramji's wife, was telling the children to leave Adele (Adele had complained of a splitting headache) for once in peace, please, and Adele had felt like the guilty one. Perhaps it was the way she looked men in the eye when she spoke, the way she wore her clothes —her T-shirts without a bra. The way she sat on the floor with her legs crossed.

By the end of the day, however, when nothing around her seemed to have changed—the house, the meals, Ramji, Sonia, Gita, and the noisy children— Adele began to think that perhaps she had dreamt the whole thing. When she asked Him if by chance during that night, He, too, had heard the barking dogs and if the barking dogs had also kept Him awake, He shook His head. He said He rarely slept anyway, and when He did sleep, He knew how to control His dreams.

Sixty-Eight

I never did tell Adele how, when I was young, I thought of nothing else. Not about school, not about books, not about clothes, later not even about boys. Each day was the same; I would spend nearly all of it, six, seven, eight hours, taking dance classes. Hour after exhausting hour, I would stand at the barre working on my extension, on my turnout. Hour after grueling hour, I would ceaselessly do the combinations in the middle of the room—*relevé, tourné, fouetté, jeté,* and again, *relevé, tourné, fouetté, jeté.*

I was so acutely conscious of my body, daily I stretched and flexed every muscle of it—to me, my body was like a machine that needed to be oiled, greased, lubricated. I was aware of every lungful of air I inhaled, then exhaled; I was aware of every morsel, every bite I put into my mouth, then swallowed—painstakingly, I had calculated every calorie, vitamin, mineral. I was equally aware of the waste—the amount I perspired, the amount (and the color) I passed—so that the slightest variation from the norm or from the previous day, any almost imperceptible change, the smallest imperfection, which was equivalent to perhaps a mosquito bite, to an ingrown hair, to a hangnail, took on, for me, the dimensions of a cancer, of an amputation, of total paralysis.

One afternoon, however—one of the last days before the weather changed—when it was so hot that most of the people had gone indoors and the beach, except for Adele and me, was nearly deserted, I could not resist showing Adele.

First, in preparation (although I told Adele that I had not done this in a long time), I went into a *demi-plié* in fifth position, my weight equally distributed on both feet—bare feet, in the hot sand—and since I was going to go to the right, my right foot was in front and my right arm was in first position, my left arm in second. I started with my right arm and, for momentum, I flung it away out to the side, to not quite second position, at the same time that I pushed off with both feet and my supporting leg (left leg) went up into *demi-pointe* and a *relevé*—harder to do in the sand since there is less turning force or torque than there is on a hard wood floor—and the working leg (the right leg) went into a *retiré* while the right arm returned to first position and was immediately joined by my left arm. My head, which was facing front, straight out to sea—I spotted the motorboat which bobbed at anchor about fifty yards away—lagged just slightly behind the turn; then I quickly spun it around back to the original position—spotting the bobbing motorboat again—an instant before my body had completed the turn. My right leg slipped behind my left leg to finish in fifth position, the same position that I began the pirouette in, and I opened both my arms out to Adele in the *offrande* position.

"It's easy. You try," I said.

Adele did.

As if she had been practicing it all her life, Adele did a perfect pirouette in the sand.

Sixty-Nine

In his dream, Howard told Nina, Adele was begging for money in some big city in India, like Bombay or Calcutta, and when Howard walked past her in the street, at first he did not recognize Adele. Adele was dressed in filthy rags, and Adele's outstretched arm was so thin it looked like a bone a dog had already picked clean. Her hands were gnarled and callused and her nails were bitten down past the quick and were bleeding. Adele's face, Howard said, was covered with hideous running sores. Her eyes were half-closed and thick with flies where pus was oozing from the lids.

Then the dream changed, the way dreams do, Howard said. The dream was filled with people from Howard's business, and people Howard had never seen before, and they were all sailing on a small cargo boat. There were horses and water buffalo tied up on the deck of the boat, and it was clear that the animals were being shipped somewhere for slaughter. It was very hot, Howard said, and the sea was very flat and gray, a little ominous, and occasionally, he could see flying fish in the water. Howard remembered that from time to time crew members would come on deck and hose down the horses and the water buffalo, and the stench that came off their steaming bodies drove everyone on the boat down below and to their cabins. One time, Howard said, in his dream, as he was rounding a corner below the deck, there was Adele as the beggarwoman again, squatting in front of the door to his cabin. "Whatever you do, don't give that woman money. Don't give her anything, if she asks you," Howard said he told someone. But in the next, so to speak, scene of his dream—as if she belonged there—Adele was stretched out with her feet crossed at the ankles on top of the berth in his cabin.

His dream reminded Howard of a film, one of those short experimental films that were only shown at festivals and that he could never quite understand.

Nina asked her father then: "What was Mom wearing? Was Mom still wearing her beggarwoman clothes while she was lying on top of the berth in your cabin, Dad?"

Howard told Nina he could not remember.

Howard said: "No. I don't know. She looked like herself again. She wasn't wearing anything—anything special, that is. Oh, come to think of it, maybe she was. She was wearing a red two-piece bathing suit."

Seventy

Never will I forget how, at first, I said I did not want her! Never will I forget how I told Nina the city was no place for a dog, especially such a big dog. Never will I forget how I told Nina that my apartment was too small, that she would be left alone all day and feel lonely. Never will I forget how I told Nina that, unlike her mother, Adele, I was not good with animals. (To be honest, I am afraid of most large animals—of horses, cows, large dogs like Great Danes and German shepherds; I am even afraid of those dogs that are trained to rescue people from avalanches—Saint Bernards!)

In addition, never will I forget how everyone warned me! How everyone said things to me like:

Mark my words, a dog is a huge responsibility!

I swear, looking after a dog is like looking after a baby!

Wait and see, a dog is going to change your life!

Seventy-One

*That is perfect. This is perfect. Perfect comes from perfect.
Take perfect from perfect, the remainder is perfect. May
peace and peace and peace be everywhere.*

—THE UPANISHADS

He said Adele had no choice.

He said Adele could never go back to her old
life.

Adele, He said, had now forgotten everything
she once knew.

Barefoot and wearing a printed cotton sari,
Adele was sitting on the clean-swept wooden floor in
the living room with her head bent down, her knees

drawn up to her chin. In the kitchen, ignoring her, the women were talking, laughing, slapping *chapatis* into shape, a child was reciting verse.

When Adele looked up, her eyes looked bluer than they had ever looked, and her eyes could look through everything—through the rattan furniture, through the glass coffee table with old magazines and a copper ashtray on it, through the shuttered windows, through the paddles of the slow-turning ceiling fan, through the pictures on the wall: a black-and-white photograph of Him with, underneath it, a burning votive candle and a jasmine lei, a watercolor landscape a friend had given Him of some bright green mountains with a rushing stream in front of them, a calendar turned to the month before last with a picture of a smiling Indian woman wearing an orchid in her hair, and finally, a framed piece of yellow silk with His name embroidered on it that Adele had forgotten (forgotten along with everything else Adele once remembered) she had long ago cross-stitched for Him.

Before, He said, Adele was just like the woman who arrives at the marketplace after dark. In the dark, she cannot see what she is buying—there are all kinds of merchandise. She hands out her money but she cannot see what people hand her in return. Blindly, she stuffs everything into her bag. When she gets home and empties her bag, she sees that what she thought was a rope is a snake, what she thought might be honey is thick black tar, what she thought was meat for eating is a rotten carcass, and so on and so forth. Not only has the woman spent all her money, she has bought herself a heap of trouble as well.

A human being entering this world, He said, was just like the woman going to market in the dark.

Adele, her short dark hair streaked with white, the curl nearly gone out of it, looking older than her years—to Howard, to Harry and Nina, to her friends, probably hardly recognizable—was very far away indeed.

Seventy-Two

*Out of the ocean like rain clouds come and travel—for
without traveling you will never become a pearl!*

—FARIDUDDIN ATTAR

Her leather pocketbook slung over her shoulder, her
small duffel bag clutched in one hand, and wearing
one of her flowered rayon skirts and the T-shirt that
had a picture of a turtle from the Okavango Delta
on it, was how Adele said she was dressed again
when she spent the entire day at the airport—
already, she had said the Bombay airport was
chaotic and crowded—going from one terminal to

the other, incapable of deciding, incapable of making up her mind.

I would be surprised too, Adele said to me, how many airlines there were she had never heard of, and I should have seen her ticket by the end of the day—should she fly Air India to Gatwick and from there change to Northwest Airlines? Or should she save a lot of money by flying standby all the way to San Francisco on Cathay Pacific? Her ticket had been stapled over so many times it was impossible to tell the name of the original carrier or whom the ticket had been issued by.

By the end of the day, too, Adele said how she knew her way around the airport practically the way she knew her way around her own house in Connecticut. She could recite for me, if I wanted her to—at the time, Adele sounded almost as if she was boasting just a little—how beginning with the west wing of the terminal, the airline departure gates were situated in the following order: Korean Air, then Japan Airlines, Singapore Airlines, Trans Australian Airlines, Thai Airways, Garuda, Qantas, Air Maroc, Royal Jordanian, and finally, Pakistan International Airlines. In addition, Adele said she knew which restaurants she could sit at the longest and where, undisturbed by porters or beggars, she could order and sip at only a cup of coffee. She knew which rest rooms were the cleanest, the most convenient—where there was an attendant, where there was plenty of toilet paper.

In the end, just as it was getting dark, Adele had finally boarded a plane, a British Airways Boeing 727, the last flight out of Bombay that night, which was leaving for London's Heathrow after first making a stop in Zurich, Switzerland. Adele was lucky, she said the plane was still parked at the gate, and lucky, too, she was sitting on the aisle and had only carry-on luggage (the duffel bag fit easily into the overhead rack), because just as they were shutting the airplane doors, Adele had grabbed her duffel bag and rushed down the aisle to the stewardess and told her that she had changed her mind. She had to get off the plane, she had to go back—back to Him.

Seventy-Three

We have our habits, we keep to our routine. When I come home in the evening, for example, first thing, rain or shine, I take her out for a walk. When we get back, I put fresh water into her bowl, pour myself a glass of cold white wine, listen to the evening news. A little later, I fix both our dinners, which we eat together—she eats much faster than I do—in the kitchen. Afterwards, I like to relax, to read or watch television. In the living room, I make myself comfortable, stretch out (I kick off my shoes, I wrap the paisley shawl around my legs), and since I do not let her jump up on the sofa—dog hairs are difficult to brush off—she lies quietly next to me on the rug. (With one hand, I can easily reach down and pat her.)

Occasionally, however—also, I am curious, can I still do it?—I put on some music ("Swan Lake" or maybe it is "Giselle") and, from the back of my closet, I get out my silk toe shoes. Then, going to stand in the hall, I support myself with both hands at the hall table, and I do a *relevé* in second position, a *sous-sus* in fifth position, an *échappé* and a *glissade* and *assemblé sur les pointes*. When I am feeling steadier and I can no longer feel the wobble in my ankles, the strain in my shoulders, I let go of the table with one hand and do a *bourrée* followed by a *jeté relevé* and a *pas de bourrée piqué*. Finally, when I feel the spring necessary to rise onto toe, I let go of the table, the makeshift barre, completely, and I do a *retiré passé*; then, still on point, I do a fast *glissade* down the hall, and just before I reach the end wall, I do a *grand jeté en avant*, landing on my front leg with my back leg in an *arabesque* while, at my heels, Lily is running after me down the hall, barking, barking, barking.

On a few evenings, I have been so tired or (I have to admit) I have drunk a glass or two too many of white wine that I have fallen asleep fully dressed (except for my shoes) lying on the sofa, with the television set still on. Later on, when all of a sudden I have woken up, I know, the way one knows these things right away (perhaps by the late-night sounds coming from the television set), that it is at least three or four o'clock in the morning. Likewise, it has happened to me that for a few moments, I have felt so disoriented —are those people really engaged in cunnilingus or are they just pretending?—that not until I have put out my hand and have felt that it is really Lily who is lying pressed up against me—she takes advantage of my falling asleep and jumps up on the sofa—have I known for sure where I am.

Seventy-Four

"You're crazy if you go in today," I said to Adele. By then, I should have known better. I should have known to save my breath.

On the last day, the waves crashing onto the beach were almost as tall as I and were an ominous translucent pale green color. The waves rose up so high that the spray reached the cliff on which the restaurant was situated. The stones at the bottom of the sea, like a giant game of dominoes going on, made a loud rackety-clackety sound of things being moved and shifted and thrown (already, the French boy had a purple bruise the size of a grapefruit on his shin where one of the stones had hit him). We had to shout to hear each other.

Red flags had been placed at intervals in the sand on the beach, but of course, Adele had paid no attention to them.

The trick, Adele said, was to get in the sea quickly, to dive through the waves before they broke on you—her father had shown her. The same thing was true of getting out. Getting out was trickier, Adele admitted. Timing was everything. One could not hesitate, not even for a split second.

One time years ago, Adele said she had been rolled by a wave so badly she had lost her bathing suit —a two-piece bathing suit like the one she was wearing that day. She had come out of the water stark naked—only she was this skinny kid and if I thought she was flat-chested now, I should have seen her then —and her father had made her go right back in the water the way she was, with nothing on. Naked.

"You should have seen my father," was the last thing Adele said to me before she went in. "My father was a great swimmer in his day—that is, before he started drinking, drinking gin.''

One by one, after what seemed to me to be a long time, longer than they had ever stayed out in the ocean before, Adele's dogs, the three Irish setters, came back in. First, strangely enough, Suzy—I recognized Suzy right away—the smallest, the most delicate of the three dogs, as if by a miracle, suddenly there she was, standing on the beach. Too tired to shake herself, she lay down on her side in the sand, her ear flapping open and exposing the yellowish-pink inside part the way it always did. Next, rolled in on a high crashing wave, I caught sight of Lily's head—by then I had seen Lily enough times, I was certain that it was Lily—just before she disappeared under again. She disappeared for such a long time that, looking all over for her in the water, I was certain that Lily must have drowned. When finally she struggled out of the ocean, Lily—I was right, it was Lily—was limping. She had torn a muscle or a ligament in her back leg. Shaking herself —nearly unbalancing herself and falling over each time she did that—Lily went to sit down on the beach next to Suzy. In response, Suzy lifted her head, feebly wagged her tail. Heidi was the last of the three dogs to swim in. As a matter of fact, after almost an hour, and after I had almost given up on her, at last I saw a small dark dot swimming in what looked like aimless circles beyond the green waves, beyond the green breakers, and for a moment, I mistook Heidi's head for Adele's.

"Adele!" I yelled.

"Adele!"

Seventy-Five

"A mistake," the man who stops me in the street says.

"Sorry," he also says. "But isn't that one of her dogs? One of the Irish setters?"

"Yes, Lily," I say.

The man then says how, at first, he had thought I was she, only now that he is standing next to me, he can see that she was a little taller than I, that she weighed five or six pounds less than I do, that her hair, too, was shorter, curlier, darker—even though it was streaked with white, only like Harry, he calls it silver —than my hair and that, finally, my eyes are brown, while her eyes were blue.

"But where is Adele, do you know?" the man, who tells me his name is Jim Baronio and that he was her neighbor in Connecticut, still wants to know.

Seventy-Six

The rivers all in Paradise
Flow with the word Allah, Allah,
And ev'ry longing nightingale
He sings and sings Allah, Allah.

— YUNUS EMRE

Everyone predicted that the weather would change, and every year, too, at that time, the sand on the beach shifted. During those days while it rained and while the high green waves sprayed and pounded the shore of the beach and the stones at the bottom of the sea rolled and crashed into each other making the familiar racket and clackety-clack sound so that no one could sleep, the sand on the beach disappeared.

Afterwards, on the first sunny day, what had happened was all too clear. Instead of the beach sloping gently down toward the sea, there was now a sharp rift. The beach dropped nearly three feet. Instead of the smooth sand at the edge of the sea, there were rough stones.

The stones made it difficult to walk into the ocean. To swim, people had to put on shoes. For fear of scraping its bottom, the motorboat could no longer be beached easily.

Then, five or six months later, just as people seemed to have forgotten and had become accustomed to it, and the stones on the beach seemed permanent, on a new moon, once again the weather changed and it began to rain. The rain beat down on the bougainvillea and the frangipani trees causing the leaves and delicate fragrant blossoms to become sodden and drop off. The rain drove away the little yellow sugar birds and made them seek shelter elsewhere. The rain leaked through the flimsy thatched roofs of the bungalows, wet the sheets on the empty beds and dripped on the unoccupied sofa cushions.

But after a few days, when the sun finally burst through the clouds and the tropical sky was its habitual brilliant blue once more, the beach, as if by a miracle, had been restored.

"You see!" one person shouted in triumph.

"What did I tell you!" a second person seconded him.

The fine white sand sloped smoothly down to the sea the way it had done before, the motorboat was bobbing gently on its mooring as if it had been there all along, people were running barefoot into the water the way they used to. The red hibiscus, the red, purple, and orange bougainvillea, the pink and white frangipani, were blooming profusely and spreading their perfume along the shore, the little yellow sugar birds hopped gracefully from table to table in the restaurant, and below on the beach, in the cove formed by the cliff, in place of the rumbling stones, lay shiny pink conch shells freshly washed up from the sea.